TIME STEALERS'
HOPE ETERNAL

P. CLAUSS

ISBN 978-1-953223-92-0 (paperback)
ISBN 978-1-954345-57-7 (digital)

This is a work of fiction. Names, characters and situations are the product of the author's imagination, except the horological associations that are named and the clocks that are mentioned in the story.

Rushmore Press LLC
1 800 460 9188
www.rushmorepress.com

Printed in the United States of America

DEDICATION

**To friends old and new,
for their support
and encouragement.**

ACKNOWLEDGEMENTS

My special thanks to Pat Holloway and Audrey Weatherly, for their unique perspectives on the story.

Also to my very patient editor, Kathy Locatelli, who once again polished up a very rough literary stone.

I also extend my heart felt gratitude to the very helpful clock and watch community on the NAWCC message boards for their recommendations and suggestions.

And my specific thanks to Shaun Clarke for all his knowledge on very old pocket watches and to point me in the direction of searching for that one specific pocket watch.

CONTENTS

PROLOGUE

He wasn't sure where the thought came from. But there he was, spying from the bushes at Master Gregory's mansion like a naughty kid.

He smiled at that thought. Of course, he was a naughty kid. He had always been naughty but had gotten away with it over the years because he could hide it so well. *Now, I'll be the one who will bring the world to its knees,* he thought as he smiled to himself.

He shifted his weight from one leg to the other as he squatted down in the shrubbery. His thoughts flitted from one image of himself in power to another. He was sure his plan would work. Everything was in place; all he needed was the Chosen One, and he would be victorious!

He had contacted his helper to inform him where the Chosen One was and for him to collect her. He saw his orders were upheld as his messenger showed up. However, his building glee was dashed when he saw the man, her own brother, tossed out empty-handed. His anger at Curtis's failure was soon cooled when he noticed a sudden scramble of activity in the stand of trees on the far edge of the property. As he watched, he became more curious as to what was going on, especially since they should have been looking for their darling wraith that he had kidnapped.

He strained his eyes, wishing he had brought binoculars, as he saw them scurry from the mansion with something in their hands, heading for the trees. He couldn't quite make out what was going on in the wooded area but thought he saw some wraith activity. He silently cursed the fact that everything was too far away.

As they came back toward the house, he saw that they were carrying handfuls of pocket watches as if they were extremely fragile. He carefully moved in closer to peek into the mansion. After looking through several windows, he found one where he could see them arrange the watches in precise rows on a massive, blanket-covered dining room table.

Suddenly, his curiosity blossomed into a desire to snatch one of them. It was as if the pocket watch he had laid his eyes on summoned him to take it away from that place. Although the draw was achingly strong, he was momentarily distracted from it after seeing Curtis' sister. Finally seeing her with his own eyes, he desired her as well. "A forever companion," he sighed wistfully to himself. He instantly longed for her to join him in his cause.

When the room emptied of people and wraiths for a brief time, the lure of the pocket watch wrenched him from his fanciful thoughts. He. Had. To. Get. That. Watch.

He expertly jimmied open the window and slid into the room. Dropping on all fours, he scurried to the table and popped up long enough to spot the pocket watch of his desires. He snatched it, stuffed it in his pocket, and slithered back out of the window.

He had just closed the window behind him when another load of watches were brought in to be laid down. The missing watch had not been noted as it was the last one placed of the previous batch. The spot looked as if it already had been empty and was the next to be filled.

Crouching down, he ran through the bushes toward his car, which was hidden at the back of the estate. He looked over his shoulder before he got in and saw that he had gotten away without anyone's having a clue something had happened.

Sliding into the driver's seat, he pulled out the pocket watch and looked it over. It was a beauty, and it was big. It looked to be solid gold making up the rounded case and heavily engraved face. The dial was further accented with a white, engraved, inner ring and twelve patches with roman numerals graved into each. He wondered if the white material was ivory. A single, ornate, gold hand apparently marked the time in hours. Not being a pocket watch collector, he didn't know the maker or age as he hefted its weight in his hand. As he admired it, he marveled at its unique beauty. But more than that, there was a strong presence. It was unlike anything he had ever sensed before.

He was curious about what could live in the small movement of a pocket watch that had such a powerful presence. But he didn't bother to dwell on the thought too long as he smiled in glee that he had snatched it out from underneath their noses. The thought of grabbing the Ultimate Time Keeper had been temporarily overshadowed by his new acquisition.

After pocketing the watch again, he started his car and sped away. The fading light of the setting sun glinted off his gold tooth.

CHAPTER ONE

Grant sat looking at the pieces of the clock. A black, wispy being floated nearby, watching him intensely. The features of the shifting, smoky-like substance were definitely female.

He had already thrown away the wood pieces that were too smashed up to be usable. He had taken the mangled movement apart and had the brass plates, gears, and other various pieces scattered over his worktable. He sighed heavily as he picked up a gear to study the missing teeth and bent up arbor. He sighed again as he set it down and picked up another piece torn up by the violence that had been inflicted on it.

Grant put the other piece down and ran his fingers through his dark, curly hair. "I don't know, Becker," he addressed the wraith, which despite the vague facial features looked anxious. "He really did some excessive damage."

The 'he' Grant referred to was the mysterious evil Keeper. He was the one who orchestrated an attack against humans by using the evil Time Wraiths he had released from the Time Keepers' vaults and other wraiths that he had controlled using mysterious silver cubes and handheld devices.

Grant sat back as he remembered the events from months ago. He shuddered to think of what would have happened to the world as a whole if the evil Keeper had been successful.

The Keepers knew that the wraiths could affect people's perception of time. This ability would create situations for people that could be distracting enough that they would make devastating mistakes. They could wreak havoc and destruction by simply causing a bus driver to go the wrong way, a nuclear technician to activate the wrong switch, the stockbroker to make the wrong move at the wrong time. The possibilities were endless. Fortunately, the Keepers had unknown champions – the Sentinels, who emerged from some of the major tower clocks around the world. They turned the tide of the battle and were currently keeping many of the evil Time Wraiths imprisoned with them.

He was pulled out of his thoughts by his ringing phone. He saw the caller was his friend and fellow Keeper. "Hey, John," he answered.

"Hey, Grant," his friend responded. "Have you heard of any Keepers getting their vaults restarted?"

"No," Grant answered glumly. "If we can figure out how he did it, we can figure out how to fix them."

"Oh, okay." The previously cheerful voice dimmed a notch. "Hey, what's up? You sound really down."

"Yeah, well, looking at Becker's clock. She's tired of the grandfather she's been camping in. She wants her house back."

"It was smashed up pretty bad," his friend sympathized. "Those pictures you sent me were really depressing. That much damage shows a lot of rage."

Grant grimaced. "I know. I'm worried what's going to happen the next time he emerges." He sighed heavily as his attention focused on what he could do at the moment, and that was trying to fix Becker's home. "I'm seeing what I can salvage from it to try to keep it as original as possible. I'm keeping an eye out for original replacement parts on Ebay."

"Tall order," his friend sympathized. "How's Charlotte and her grandfather?"

Instantly, Grant felt physical pain through his chest. His heart hurt badly with wrenching emotions. This natural question brought to mind something that he was trying not to think about.

His extended silence alerted his friend that something was not right. But before he had a chance to press for information, Grant finally confessed, "We haven't spoken for a few weeks."

"What did you do?" John asked; his tone was half joking but with serious undertones.

"What?!" Grant sat up rigidly as he gripped the phone tightly. "Why do you assume I did something wrong?" he blurted, reflecting his anger and hurt.

"Ah, it was something you didn't do…" John left it hanging in the air. Grant's prickly reaction didn't sway him. They had been friends for centuries, and he knew it was his right to know. He wanted to help his friend if he could.

"John, quit with your speculating." Grant slumped in his chair and sighed. His reflexive anger dissipated quickly and left him tired.

His request was ignored as his friend continued to pry for information. "What happened, Grant? I thought things were good between you two."

"Oh, they were great." Grant smiled with a happy memory. "But I made a mistake."

"What?" the voice was insistent. "Date her friend?"

"No! Look, John, just stop!" Grant wanted to be left alone. He was tempted to hang up but didn't want to be rude to his friend. He was trying to think of something, anything else, to talk about. The broken-up clock was forgotten as he placed his face in his hands with his elbows on the worktable.

"Need to tell me," his friend warned. "I can think of all sorts of scenarios."

"Okay, stop." Grant took a deep breath. He gave up. He could see John would not give up until he knew the details. "She found out how old I am."

A long pause told Grant that John knew the seriousness of that revelation. He was almost as old as Grant and was aware how someone would react to that information. "How did she find out?" his friend asked quietly.

"I told her," Grant confessed. "I mean, there is supposed to be truth in a relationship. Right?"

"True," John paused for a moment. "But wasn't that too early for that bit of truth in the relationship?"

"Ah, well, we were discussing history and I slipped and gave a first-person account of a famous event. She latched onto that."

"Which event? Was I there?"

"Yeah, you were there." Grant muttered. "The Boston tea party."

"Oh!" John exclaimed. "I hadn't thought about that in years! That was fun. Better than the protests in the '60s."

Grant shook his head and smiled. He sat up and leaned back into his chair. He didn't interrupt John as he brought up events from their shared past. Only John could bring things up to make him smile even with the way he felt. At least, it was distracting his friend from his situation with Charlotte.

But he found he was not off the hook. When John finally stopped tripping down memory lane, he asked Grant, "So, is it a done deal or is she simply stepping back to process the facts?"

"She said that she is processing the facts," Grant muttered into the phone. "Weldon is trying to help, but I don't know what's going to happen."

"Do you think she is safe?"

"I hope. She knows he is still out there." He paused to think. "I hope she's careful," he muttered in deep concern as John's question drove it home that he was no longer near enough to her to watch over her and to make sure she remained cautious.

"Even if he never bothers her again, we still need to find him," John stated seriously. "He is a huge risk to the world with his abilities."

"Agreed," Grant replied. A movement caught his eye. Becker, the wraith, was waving a hand at him. She was agitated. "Well, Becker's getting mad at me," he sighed

"Batting a thousand with the females, dude," John quipped with a laugh.

"Thanks for the solidarity, dude," Grant grumbled, then warmed up his voice as he smiled. "Thanks for calling," he said, truly appreciating that his friend had called.

"Don't be a stranger," John said, then disconnected.

Grant set his phone down and started to seriously consider what to do with the clock movement. John's phone call had helped to get him back on track by being able to share his secret grief to someone who truly understood. He knew he had to separate what he could do from that which he could only wait to see what would happen.

He was fully engaged with the reconstruction and restoration project when he heard the chime on the clock shop door sound. He had a customer. He carefully set down the verge he had been studying and stepped out of his workshop into the showroom.

"Hi! Welcome!" Grant greeted the older man who was peering around as if he was nearsighted. "How may I help you?"

"I am looking for a grandfather clock with chimes," the older man said quietly. Grant saw as the customer turned toward him that his eyes squinted and his brow furrowed as he tried to see him.

"I have several out on the floor to look at. Or if you have one in mind, I could possibly find it for you."

"Oh, son," the older man started, "you see, the sound of the clock is what is going to matter rather than how it looks."

Grant pondered the older man's words. The specific request was unusual.

The older man noted his silence and leaned toward him to confide with him. "You see, I was recently diagnosed with macular degeneration." He peered intently at Grant's face. "I am going blind." A grandfather chimed the quarter hour. He perked up and looked around, trying to locate the clock.

He looked back up at Grant in his nearsighted fashion. "My family had a grandfather clock. I loved the sound of the clockworks and the chiming throughout the day." His face fell with a memory of sorrow. He sighed heavily. "We lost the clock to a fire. All the family was safe but the house burned to the ground. Out of everything we lost that day, we mourned the loss of the clock."

Grant gently steered him by the arm to the grandfather that had chimed. He felt the old man's hurt. It was similar to many stories he had heard over the years.

"When I was in my teens," the gent continued his story as they walked, "I wanted to have another grandfather clock. But I was moving around too much at that time. Then when I married, my wife wouldn't stand for such a clock." They stopped in front of the grandfather. "She said it would take too much room and make too much noise."

Grant wondered how much detail the elderly man could see. He debated whether he should describe the imposing, carved wooden case, silvered face with moon dial, and large lyre pendulum when the old man placed a hand on the case.

"Can I hear the cycles of chiming and strike?" he asked quietly.

"Sure," Grant replied as he opened the side door at the top of the case that gave access to the mechanism. As he triggered it to cycle through the half hour, three-quarter hour, and hour chime and let it strike the hour, he watched the expression on the elderly man's face.

"Is this a tubular chime?" the customer asked as he cocked his head to listen intently to the very quiet tick-tock as the lyre pendulum barely swung in its compartment.

"No, this one has chime rods," Grant answered.

"I see. That must be the difference," the older man sighed. "It sounds so close to my old family clock. As I remember, there was more of a resonance in the sound."

"Ah. I believe you may like this one," Grant responded as he led the older man to another clock, an early 1900s, tubular chime grandfather clock. It also had an embossed face with a moon dial. Although the wooden case was less ornate, it had an elegant simplicity. "See how this one sounds." He tripped the mechanism to activate the chime and strike. He was rewarded by a rapt expression on the old man's face.

"Yes, that sounds like him." He peered closely at the dark wood finish and the glass in front of the dial as well as the lower compartment housing the pendulum and weights. He raised an arm to feel the rounded top of the case and down the smooth sides. "I believe this is the same clock or very similar."

Grant contemplated the clock's maker and the model. He could see possibilities of a match with the time it was manufactured to the old man's story. "It could be, if the fire happened when you were very young."

"It did, my fellow, it did." The elder gent smiled, showing too perfect teeth, as he fumbled for his wallet with arthritic hands to pull out a credit card. He handed it to Grant. "Make sure to add delivery and set up," he said as he grinned brightly while he stared lovingly at what he considered was now his clock.

Grant held the credit card dumbfounded. "Don't you want to know the cost?"

"It doesn't matter." The elderly man stroked the clock case as he leaned over to listen to the slow tick-tock of the clock. "I have enough money to spend." As he continued to listen to the clockworks, he smiled and muttered more to himself than to Grant, "I have no one. She didn't want kids either. I guess they would've made too much noise as well." He sighed heavily as Grant turned away. "But now, I found my clock."

Tears sprung unbidden to Grant's eyes as pain struck his heart. Through his long life, he was well acquainted with loneliness and regret.

He walked to the counter to pull out his pad to run the credit card. From past experience, if people didn't want to know the price, they usually were shocked when the credit transaction was declined. Because he was half expecting it to be declined, he felt guilty for thinking that way and was happy when it went through. He was glad he could provide the older man his dream clock so he could have it for the rest of his life. He briefly had a thought of what would happen to the clock when he died. That wasn't his business, but he worried whether that magnificent Herschede would be treated well in the future. He knew that with care, it could last for another hundred plus years.

He took the pad over to the old man. "Please sign with your finger," he said as he held it out. "I'll need the address if you could write it down as well."

The old man smiled as he scrawled his signature and address on the screen. "These electronic gadgets make it fun to spend money," he cackled merrily.

"Mr. Thomas," a male voice came from the door. Grant had been so involved in his thoughts of the older gent that he hadn't heard the door chime. "Are you ready to go back? The others are ready and waiting in the van."

"Oh, Roger!" the old man exclaimed with excitement as he waved the man over. "I found him! I found the right clock!"

The stocky, bald man walked over to where they were standing as he smiled broadly. "Finally, sir! I am so happy for you." He faced the indicated grandfather clock and looked it over while he pursed his lips in thought. Grant could tell he was estimating dimensions.

The older man started to get worried at the silence of his companion. "It is okay, isn't it? It looks good? It will fit?"

The other man sighed. "Sir, it is beautiful! Magnificent! But, I don't see how we can fit it in your room."

"Oh, that!" The elder man grinned as his eyes sparkled. "I guess I forgot to mention. This is for the sitting room. So all can enjoy!" He leaned toward the companion. "I already cleared it with the powers that be."

Roger smiled in relief. "That is good, sir!" He looked the clock over again. "All the residents will enjoy him." He looked over at Grant. "No one has to pick it up?"

Grant shook his head. "I will deliver it." He looked down at the address. "This is the right address?" he whispered. As he showed it to the companion, the older gent was heading for the door.

"Yes," Roger said quietly. "Thanks for checking." He turned to watch to make sure Mr. Thomas made it through the shop door without assistance.

"I know sometimes there is confusion where they live at times," Grant offered.

The other man laughed softly as he looked back at him. "So, true. However, Mr. Thomas is very sharp. He joined our community so he would have people around. And for the activities to help him keep busy."

Grant nodded slowly; he knew how wanting companionship felt. He looked up to see Roger looking around the shop.

"This is fascinating," he murmured. "I need to come back and see what you have. I never thought about owning a mechanical clock, but the sound is rather relaxing."

"You're welcome anytime," Grant replied as he smiled. He had seen many people come into his clock shop with other clock enthusiasts and become enchanted with the ambiance of ticking clocks. He thought of the policemen he had talked to over the years who were hired to guard the timepieces at various clock shows. Many would be fascinated by all the clocks they would see and would comment on the sounds of the clockworks, chiming and striking that would fill the nighttime silence of the big showrooms.

Roger drew his attention back to the present. "Well, that will have to be another day. Need to go and get our shoppers back to their home," he said cheerfully as he waved to Grant and left.

As he returned to the counter to put the pad back in its place, Grant was deep in his thoughts about Mr. Thomas and Roger, the cheerful companion. "That is good," Grant mused, "for the elderly to have people who enjoy helping them." He was writing the address down on a delivery order when a soft voice startled him.

"You are very kind and gentle to the elderly," a woman's voice spoke from the far end of the counter.

He startled as he looked up to see Charlotte. He gave her a long, lingering look of admiration at her loosely curled, tousled, dark blonde hair, bright blue eyes, and fair complexion. A lump rose in his throat and prevented him from speaking as his pleasant surprise morphed from happy expectation to fear. Her neutral expression gave no clue as to what she was thinking.

CHAPTER TWO

"You know, you are much older than he is," she observed quietly as she looked toward the shop door and back to him. "You're in much better shape for your age."

"There, but for the grace of God, go I," Grant quoted.

Charlotte nodded solemnly as she pulled her lower lip between her teeth thoughtfully. "And a Time Keepers' clockworks room," she added quietly. She was about to say something else when Becker came into the showroom and started to fly around her excitedly. "Hi, Becker!" She redirected her attention to the wraith. "Is he working on your home?"

Grant groaned as he closed his eyes. He didn't have to see the wraith's expressions to know what she was mentally communicating to Charlotte in visual images. He opened his eyes to see Becker floating in front of Charlotte, hands on hips, while her head nodded as she seemed to speak furiously. He closed his eyes again. When he dared to open them, he saw what he had expected. Charlotte was staring at him with hard, stormy eyes. "Look, she seemed happy in the grandfather," he pleaded for her to understand with his hands spread open in front of him. "It wasn't until recently that she indicated she wanted her clock back."

"It is her home!" Charlotte shot back.

"I know!" he returned just as forcefully. "I didn't smash it up!"

Charlotte blushed; she broke off eye contact as her expression softened. Grant watched as it changed into a pensive worry. "Any word on the evil Keeper?" she asked quietly.

Grant's shoulders slumped as he leaned against the counter. He was relieved the focus had been redirected from the tension between them. The evil Keeper was a very different kind of stress that brought them together against an outside force.

"The Keepers have banded together. This is the tightest I've ever seen the group throughout all the centuries." He winced when he let "centuries" slip out, then relaxed when he saw she was too focused on news of the evil Keeper to react. He continued, "Everyone is searching for him. No one seems to know who he is. We are beginning to think he was an unrecognized Keeper." He heard all the clocks in the shop striking twelve o'clock. "Would you like to go out for lunch?" he asked as he started to walk toward the shop door to lock it.

Charlotte didn't see him wince again when she softly replied, "No."

Standing in front of the door, he hesitated as he turned back toward her. "You need to leave?" He tried to keep the catch out of his voice. He hadn't seen her for months. *Is a brief visit all I'm going to get?* he silently wondered.

She straightened up and smoothed out her clothes as she met his eyes. "Actually, I was hoping you had a little something here. I just don't want to go out somewhere public."

As Grant turned again to lock the door and flip the 'Open' sign to 'Closed for lunch', his thoughts spun. *Should I be happy? Should I be sad?* He wasn't sure what this meant. He wasn't sure if he could eat. He turned back toward her with a smile. "I don't have much but I'm happy to share whatever we can find!"

She returned his smile, then turned to go through the curtain into the back room. "Ah, I see you've upgraded," she said as she studied the Keurig on the counter, a microwave, and a full refrigerator and oven. She also noted that the table and chairs had been refinished.

"Thanks to your grandfather," Grant replied as he pulled out one of the chairs by the table for her to sit on. "He also sends one of his maids once a week to clean this room and my upstairs apartment."

"He has?" Charlotte remarked as she sat down. She was obviously surprised by all the news. "He never told me anything."

Grant sat across from her. Not wanting to meet her eyes at that moment, he placed his hands on the table and examined them as he continued, "I kept telling him not to. But he was so insistent. I gave up and tried to enjoy his generosity." He looked up into her face, ready to see her expression regarding what he had to say. "I have really missed you."

Charlotte smiled, then let it fall away. "I think I have missed you," she started quietly. "You see, my life has been so drastically changed, I'm not sure of my feelings."

Grant sat back, his attention fully on her. He was glad she was opening up to him after all the silent months. But he feared what she was going to say. He forced himself to put all those thoughts aside and tried to park his thoughts and emotions in neutral as he heard her out.

She leaned toward him to raise a hand to his face, then let it drift to the table top. "You have lived with the knowledge of the wraiths for a long time," she started. Grant nodded, urging her to continue. "You were the one who helped me understand that I wasn't crazy and that I'm a part of something much larger than I could ever imagine." Grant nodded again.

Charlotte licked her lips before meeting his eyes again. "We dealt with a nearly catastrophic event together." She paused. "We made an awesome team!" She smiled brightly, but briefly, at the memory.

Grant smiled in response as he, too, thought they worked well together. Her next words dampened but didn't extinguish the flame of hope. "But," her voice lowered as she studied her wringing hands. "Is that enough for a true relationship between a woman and man?"

He was so intent on her and trying to figure out how to reply that he didn't notice the room filling with wraiths until he caught movement in his peripheral vision. "Hey!" he exclaimed as he looked up to see the cloud-like crowd of shadowy beings near the ceiling. They all were looking back and forth between him and Charlotte.

Charlotte also looked up and jumped in surprise. She hadn't noticed them gathering, either. "Hey, guys!"

Grant really didn't want onlookers and tempered his anger at the intruders. "Will you all go back to your clocks? This is between us." When no one moved, Grant looked for Becker. "Becker, please?" he pleaded, thinking that they should listen to her. After a few moments, he saw her communicating with them. Reluctantly, the group broke up and drifted away. When the room was cleared of wraiths, Grant sighed, "Just like kids."

"Do you want kids?"

The softness of the statement had nothing to do with the impact it made on Grant. It cut through him like a knife. He met her eyes, then looked down at his hands. Clearing his throat, he said, "Yes, I do." He raised his eyes to hers to gauge her reaction. "I just don't know if I can father any."

Charlotte nodded slightly." Have you ever been married?" she asked softly. With her expression earnest but intense, Grant saw she seemed afraid of the answer.

Grant met her eyes and smiled gently. "No, I have never." Instantly, he was flooded with all the loneliness he had experienced over the centuries. The looking on as couples married, grew older together, and died. His unrequited desire to have such a relationship but not able to because of his calling, his duty.

Suddenly, he had to move, to do something to distract himself from the whirlpool of long pent-up emotions. He pushed off the table to go to the refrigerator. "Let me fix something for lunch. Coffee?"

"Yes," came the soft answer. With his back turned, he couldn't see her thoughtful expression as she watched him. "Do you have hazelnut?"

"Yes." He rummaged around as he smiled at her over his shoulder. He had successfully shut down his internal turmoil yet again. Instead he focused his thoughts on how happy he was that he had gotten the hazelnut K cups for her. He had done it in case she ever came back. He started the Keurig and pulled out food items from the refrigerator. "Sandwich?" he asked as he looked over what he had.

"That will be good." She watched him for a bit, then sighed as she looked down at her hands.

"I'll lay out the fixings. You can assemble yours the way you want."

"Okay, thank you."

He quickly sliced the onion and tomato. He placed those alongside the containers of meat and cheese with mustard, mayo, and bread. Once it was all laid out, he bowed to her and waved an arm to the counter. "After you, my lady."

"Ah, so gallant," she said as she smiled.

Grant watched her as she stood up and walked over to the counter. He was glad that she seemed more relaxed. He hoped she hadn't noticed his previous internal battle. *Maybe things are going better than I think?* he wondered hopefully.

They fixed their plates and sat down at the table. After they had a few bites, Grant felt that he should explain what Keepers had to deal with in relationships. He had a firm hand on his emotions and felt that he shouldn't hide the brutal facts. "When I was first found to be a Keeper," he said as he laid his sandwich on the plate, "one of the older ones warned me about relationships." He folded his hands over the plate as his elbows rested on the table. He watched Charlotte put down her sandwich and chew thoughtfully as she listened to him. "He had seen his wife grow old and die."

She swallowed. "He could have chosen not to use the clockworks room," she stated, indicating the room specially built by the wraiths for Keepers so they would not grow old and die. It was based on anti-time so that it was also a place wraiths couldn't go into. This provided Keepers with a shelter from evil wraiths.

"True." Grant looked away toward the curtain. He figured the wraiths were listening in from somewhere. "But responsibility of taking care of the wraiths supersedes that."

"Ah." She nodded as she looked down at her plate. She looked up and met his gaze. "You have your wraiths, Papa has his wraiths, John has his wraiths, but I don't have anyone."

He sat back as he remembered how the massive tower clock wraith, the Sentinel, emerged. He was sure it was because of her. He thought of how many of the wraiths he had seen interact with her, deferred to her. They seemed to talk more directly to her instead of using basic telepathic imagery as with any other Keeper. "Charlotte." He leaned forward with his arms on the table toward her. He watched her intently as he spoke. "You have all the wraiths under your care." Although he stated the fact quietly, she drew back as if he had hit her. "You are the Ultimate Time Keeper. You are the one stated in the prophecy written by the First Time Keeper."

Charlotte ran a trembling hand over her face to rub her eyes. Then she brought both hands up to hide her face. After a deep, shaking sigh, she dropped them to her lap. She met his eyes. "It was all so unreal. I needed someone to remind me of my new reality. Thank you."

Grant nodded at her as he sat back in his chair, keeping his eyes on her. He wanted to ask her where he stood. He wanted to blurt out that since she was a Keeper, they could live a long and happy life together. He wanted to know if she wanted to marry, if she wanted children. He wanted the uncertainty to end. He wanted to know at that moment if he had a future with her. The feelings he had a few minutes ago, the ones he had thought he had caged up, started to break out again. Through the whirlwind of his thoughts and the roller coaster ride of his emotions, he forced his lips to stay clamped shut. He pushed the loneliness back into its cage. He didn't want to blow his chances by being too pushy or looking too desperate.

She looked at him with a long, lingering gaze. At first, her expression registered confusion, then resignation. She glanced at her watch and said, "I need to go." She stood up, her half-eaten sandwich forgotten. He stood up as well, feeling uncertain of what was happening. "I wanted to…" She met his eyes, "I wanted to see you again before I leave."

"Leave?" The word slipped out, sounding wretched and tortured, before Grant could stop it.

She picked up on his reaction and stepped over to him. "It's temporary." She gave him a quick hug.

He wanted to clamp his arms around her, bury his face in her hair, and never let her go. But when she moved away, he let his arms fall to his sides. He didn't ever want her to feel trapped or caged in.

"Papa and I are going to tour the European tower clocks. At least, the ones we know haven't been converted."

"Lobotomized," Grant muttered. He was regaining control of his inward battle, so he could speak more normally.

"What?" she asked as her face relaxed to show lively curiosity. "Did you say lobotomized?"

Grant smiled as they moved into safer waters." Yes." He relaxed as he walked with her through the curtain. His quick eyes noted the rears and feet of the wraiths as they jumped back into their clocks. "Many advocates of the tower clocks consider them lobotomized when you have the mechanical mechanism being driven by a step motor."

"Oh, I see," she smiled. "That is an apt term. That would take the personality out of the clock."

"And likely keep it from being inhabited by a Sentinel." He turned to her as they reached the door of the shop. "That is what you are actually doing, correct?"

She smiled brightly at him. "That is true. There are ulterior motives to our tour. But after seeing that clock in the courthouse tower, I wanted to see more of them. They are fascinating mechanisms."

Grant smiled and nodded. "You are so right!" He shifted from one foot to the other. "I wouldn't mind seeing more myself," he hinted baldly.

Charlotte considered him seriously as she put a hand lightly on his chest. He was sure she could feel his heart pounding in anticipation of her answer. "Grant," she started, then stopped as she gazed into his eyes. "Not this time," she said quietly as her eyes smiled into his.

At first, he knew his heart had to have stopped when he heard the negative but then restarted when he heard the rest of her words.

"I need to do this with Papa," she continued quietly.

He could accept that she wanted time with a family member, as long as she wasn't feeling as if she had to escape from him.

He tried to smile back as he nodded. She studied his face once more before she turned toward the door. "It will give me more time to think," she said. "I will call you when I get back."

He nodded mutely as she stepped through the doorway, letting the glass door close slowly behind her. He wanted to ask more questions about her itinerary and how long she was going to be gone, but he didn't want her to misinterpret his concern as being intrusive. Then he thought of the evil Keeper, and worry hit him like a sledge hammer.

He opened the door and stepped out as she was getting to her car. "Charlotte," he called to her. She looked back at him. Her expression was unreadable. "Please be careful. There are enemies out there."

She relaxed as she smiled reassuringly. "I will remember." She looked around, then stepped up to him. After she gently laid a hand on his arm, she leaned in. "Papa is taking some of his wraiths with us."

"I doubt that he could hold them back," Grant smiled tightly but nonetheless felt relieved.

She patted his arm and got into her car. Waving out of her side window, she drove off. Grant waved at her until she turned the corner and was out of view.

He slowly turned and walked back into the shop. After closing the door, he flipped the sign back to 'Open.' Walking back to the counter, he ignored the wraiths poking their heads out of their clocks to watch him as he sat down to wait for customers and brood.

CHAPTER THREE

Months passed by. By day, Grant was busy with repairing customers' clocks or restoring clocks of all kinds and selling them. By night, he discussed information gathered by the other Keepers worldwide concerning the evil Keeper, trying to restart the vaults, and ways to secure their clockwork rooms.

One day, a wraith came through the shop window. Grant saw him while he was talking to a customer about a clock repair. He noticed that the wraith greeted and met with Becker, who had come out of her clock that Grant had finally fully restored. After he finished up with the customer and waited until he left, he went over to see what was going on. The two wraiths seemed agitated, and the other ones started to emerge out of their clocks and gather around them.

Something big is going on, he thought as he watched all the other wraiths start to act agitated. He took a longer look at the visiting wraith. "Grant?" he asked, suddenly fearful. Grant, the wraith, was Weldon's primary. "Becker?" He tried to get his wraith's attention. "What is going on?"

When she turned to him, he could see she was furious and fearful. That was when he knew it was about Charlotte. "Becker!" He needed to know what happened. When she turned away from him, he grabbed for her. As his hand passed through the body of mists and shadows, he knew he had seriously screwed up as he felt the full impact of time slowing to a stop before he completely blacked out.

He awoke face to face with Becker as she floated above, within inches from him. He moved his head side to side as he tried to focus on any of the nearby clocks. Once he could see one of the clock faces, he was relieved to see he hadn't lost hours of time.

When Becker saw he was awake and aware, she started to wave her hands as she tried to communicate something to him.

He held his hand up. He had a sharp, pounding headache like a hangover. "Sorry, Becker. It was my fault." She crossed her arms in front of her chest and nodded vigorously at him.

"Now, can you tell me what's going on?" he asked as he slowly stood up and made his way to the counter. After sitting behind it, he rested his head in his hands. Squinting his eyes in pain, he looked at her as he waited for a response.

Becker and Grant, the wraith, pointed to his phone. He picked it up and saw that Weldon had been trying to call him. He glanced up at the wraiths fearfully, then nervously tapped Weldon's name to call him back.

The phone rang before his call could go through. Weldon's name flashed on the screen. Grant answered the phone hastily, almost dropping it as he lifted it to his ear. "What is happening?" he asked tersely.

Just as tersely, Weldon responded, "Grant there?" Grant knew he was asking about his wraith.

Grant softened his tone. From those few words, he sensed the gentleman's anxiety. "Yes, he is. I am sorry, sir. It's Charlotte, isn't it?"

"Yes." The older man calmed down in response, his voice crackling with sorrow.

"What happened? He hasn't had a chance to tell me anything, but my wraiths are all upset," Grant said quickly so that Weldon knew he didn't know what was going on yet. As he spoke, he shut down his feelings. He had to before he drowned in them. He needed facts. He wanted to know details as quickly as possible. He needed to work on a plan.

"She's been kidnapped," Weldon started. "At first, I thought she had gone to the store but didn't leave a note. Then, I tried to call her and couldn't get her."

"How long have you been out of touch?" Grant asked hopefully, thinking that maybe the older man was just panicked.

"Twenty-four hours." It was whispered, but Grant heard it clearly.

Panic shot through him. He couldn't keep fear at bay much longer. "Any ransom demands? Any unknown wraith about?" He rapidly fired the questions at him.

The older man drew a deep breath. "No, Grant. She is simply gone."

"She wouldn't do that voluntarily," Grant thought out loud. "Where are you?"

"No, she wouldn't." A pause. "We are in England. I have contacted the local police. I am not hopeful."

"Have you contacted any Keepers over there?"

"Grant, you are our link to the community. I trust they know about us by now?"

"Yes," Grant responded quickly as he remembered when he broke the news. He had found the opportunity to tell the other Keepers during an online meeting. They had been relating their experiences on 'The Day of the Wraith', as they had named the event. They had also been discussing how to develop ways of finding the evil Keeper.

When this subject came up, he related his experience with the evil Keeper, making sure to tell them all the details. With this as a launching point, he broke the news of a female Keeper and an unknown, elderly Time Keeper. Grant knew that when they were shocked into silence, it was because of the announcement of the emergence of a female Keeper. When the shock wore off, their reactions varied. Many didn't believe him, some were put out, and others were cheerful that maybe, at last, they could have companions.

"They both need a clockworks room," Piers observed logically when the initial fervor died down.

"And a vault," offered a Keeper from Ohio.

"Definitely a clockworks room," Grant had replied. "Not sure about a vault. After all, none of ours are working."

"Well," said a Keeper in a strong Scottish brogue, "this could help us find the problem with our vaults. If a new vault doesn't work, the vaults need to be re-engineered. If it does work, the problem is in the plumbing of the other vaults."

Grant was brought out of his memories when he heard Weldon's voice over the phone asking, "What can we do?"

"I will contact the European Keepers," he answered. "Where in England are you right now?"

"In London."

"Have you been able to see Big Ben yet?"

"Not yet. We were getting the necessary permissions. We are running out of time. They are going to shut it down for major renovations soon."

"Right," Grant said as stood up and started to pace, running his fingers through his hair. The shutdown of Big Ben, the name of the bell for the Great Clock in Elizabeth Tower at the Palace of Westminster but used as a nickname for the entire structure, didn't concern him, only the fact of Charlotte's being missing did. "How many wraiths are with you?"

"Just a few," the old man whispered fearfully. "I think Grant went back to get the others."

"Many of them are still guarding the pocket watches," Grant muttered.

"That is true," Weldon answered. "I thought they would have emerged by now."

"I know, so did I," Grant agreed as his mind was sifting through options of what he could do about Charlotte's disappearance. "I will send some of mine to you." He considered the forces he could tap. "I will send Ansonia over to the colonel's and see if some of them could help." He glanced at Becker. She was hovering near him as she glared at him intensely. "Becker will go over to you as well." He thought that would make her happy, but she continued to glare at him with her shadowy, skeletal arms across her chest. "What?" he mouthed to her and tried to contact her telepathically. She wouldn't respond. "What?" he repeated out loud.

"What, what?" Weldon asked suspiciously from the phone.

"Oh, sorry." Grant turned his back to the wraith. "Becker is being testy. She's not telling me what's bothering her, but she's not happy."

Weldon was silent for a moment. "Grant, what do you feel about my granddaughter?" the old man asked slowly, with quiet intensity.

The question brought Grant up short. He had not expected that kind of reaction. "Um," he muttered as he paced more quickly around the show room, rubbing his face. "I'm scared for her. I'm angry that something has happened. I'm frustrated that I feel helpless and not sure what to do." He expelled a deep breath as he felt he had given an honest response to the question. So he was mystified by the heavy silence on the line. He was further perplexed when Becker swooped around him to hover in front of his face — glaring even more fiercely.

"What do you want?" he blurted mainly to Becker but also to Weldon. He heard a sigh from the other end.

"Grant," the old man started. "Why aren't you coming over here to help search. I know you love her. That's obvious to everyone, even if you don't admit it."

Grant's jaw dropped in surprise, then snapped closed tightly. He felt tears prick his eyes and his face flush. He was glad Weldon couldn't see him. He wanted to drive a fist through the wall to try to hide the pain he was feeling. But he couldn't for fear of knocking a clock off the wall. Instead he involuntarily let loose a guttural groan of anguish.

"What is wrong with you?" Weldon demanded over the phone. "What was that noise?"

"Master Gregory," Grant croaked out with deep emotion. His attempt to hide what he felt was failing miserably, especially with the fact that Charlotte was missing. He had to face the depth of what he was feeling. "Your granddaughter wants nothing to do with me," he said painfully as the confession tore away the frail bandage with which he had patched up his wounded heart. He hadn't heard a word from her since her visit before she left. Over that time, he had determined that she had rejected him completely. "She does not want to see me. Therefore, I will conduct whatever efforts I can from here to find her." The sorrow of broken hopes and dreams flooded over him, almost causing him to miss Weldon's reply.

"Grant," the voice spoke from thousands of miles away. "Grant!" the other man's voice barked out of the phone speaker, insisting on a response. "Grant, listen to me!"

Grant had sat down on a stool and hunched over as he tried to gather the tatters of his self-esteem and emotions together again. Finally, he was able to respond. "Yes?" he whispered hoarsely. He didn't know what he expected to hear, but it wasn't what Weldon said.

"Grant, you idiot!" Weldon exclaimed crisply. "She loves you. She needed time to get her bearings in this new world she is an important part of."

"There are other Keepers whom she may want to be with more than me," he croaked, stubbornly refusing to believe she actually loved him. "After all, they're all male. I don't doubt many of them are angling for her since she is the only female Keeper."

"Oh, my..." Weldon took a deep breath. "You dolt!" he exploded.

Grant's head shot up. He couldn't believe the mild-mannered gentleman could shout that loud. He could feel the waves of anger through the phone. He met Becker's eyes. She was nodding in agreement as was Grant, the wraith.

"Just because she pushed you away for space doesn't mean you tuck tail and run," the old man continued to shout. "As old as you are, you know nothing about women!"

CHAPTER FOUR

A fully chastised and worried Grant boarded a plane the next morning. Final destination - London.

The night before, he had contacted the Keepers worldwide to inform them about Charlotte's disappearance and that he would be heading to London the next day. He was surprised that so many had expressed concern over someone they hadn't met yet. As the conversation expanded, he came to realize that word had been passed around through the wraiths of the significant part she had played on the 'Day of the Wraith.' Several Keepers confirmed that their wraiths considered her to be the Ultimate Time Keeper. They also offered to help in any way they could. Many of them shared his worries that their enemy had her.

The local wraiths in and around his small town had banded together. Some chose to go with him and the wraiths that were chosen by Becker to be part of her team. The others split themselves up between guarding the clock shop and helping guard the pocket watches at Weldon's mansion. Grant had boarded the plane feeling that they were as prepared as they could be.

After an uneventful flight, he stepped out of the tunnel leading from the plane into Heathrow airport. He wandered through the area as the other passengers were greeted by friends and loved ones. Those that carried briefcases were met by other suits and escorted away. He scanned the crowd and saw no one who was familiar. He decided to claim his baggage, and then he would try to call Weldon. At least he would find out where he needed to tell a taxi to go.

He was a little disappointed. He had told Weldon and the European Keepers when he would be coming. *And they didn't bother to make sure someone was here to meet me.* Soon he shrugged his shoulders and laughed quietly at his stupidity for thinking he was that important. Looking around, he decided to consider it all as an adventure. Suddenly, he remembered why he was in London. His face fell as the worry and fear for Charlotte's safety came back and overshadowed his mind.

He grabbed his bag and headed toward the outside. He made sure to follow the exit signs through the unfamiliar structure. Plodding along with the crowd as he pulled his suitcase behind him, he became lost in his dark thoughts. A movement caught his eye to snap him back into the present.

Becker was waving her shadowy arm in front of him. She floated just above the mass of people so that he had to look up to see her. She pointed in a direction and beckoned him to follow her. Weaving through the crowd of people, he kept his eyes on her until he stepped outside into a mild English day. She kept gesturing for him to follow. He complied until he was out of the crowd and climbing onto a grassy area. There he found a crowd of grim-faced Keepers along with Weldon. The sky above them appeared thunderous and stormy because of the mass of wraiths that had gathered. It was there and then that he knew who was important and would bind the Keepers into a cohesive group, and that was Charlotte. The sudden revelation clarified to him that she was not only a spokesperson for the alien race but a unifying presence for all those who took care of them.

How could she possibly love me? I am nobody. Grant thought to himself as he stepped into the crowd to greet the Keepers.

A brief meeting in the open air was to decide how to dispatch the wraiths. The local Keepers showed Grant and Weldon the map of the area. Each one vaguely pointed to indicate places that had been searched, either physically by themselves or by the wraiths.

"She may not be in London anymore," one Keeper observed in a clipped British accent.

"That is true," stated a red-headed Keeper in a broad Scottish brogue. "She could be anywhere in England, Scotland, or Wales by now."

"Or even across the channel," a dark-haired, stocky Keeper stated in his thick German accent.

Weldon paced around in irritation while they talked. "She could be anywhere in the world," he muttered darkly.

Grant stood rooted to the spot. He heard all the voices but was too overwhelmed to focus. He knew he had to organize something structured out of the chaos. Suddenly, inspiration struck him out of the blue.

He held up a hand to everyone muttering and milling about. When he had their attention, he looked up into the mass of wraiths. "Becker! Grant! Colonel!" He knew he was gambling with the last one but was awarded with three wraiths that separated themselves from the others to float before him. One of them saluted him. "I thought you might be here," he said as he nodded to the wraith, the leader of the military-acting ones that they had rescued from Curtis' control at the Colonel's mansion.

"I know you three." He nodded to each one. "You know how to organize and command." They nodded back to him. "Find others with similar gifts." He gestured to those above them. "Break up into groups and partition off areas for each group to search in a systematic fashion."

He stopped suddenly as another thought hit him and felt like kicking himself. "Ansonia!" he shouted. Another wraith broke away to join the other three. "You found Becker when she was kidnapped." The wraith nodded. "Help them organize a search for Charlotte." Ansonia nodded to the other three. When he joined them, they floated away as a group as they made movements indicating that they were communicating with each other. As he watched, they entered into the cloud of wraiths, and the disorganized milling about of shadows started to become organized.

The other Keepers watched the activity with great interest, some with mouths dropped open in astonishment.

"How did you know they would do that?" asked a local Keeper with a cockney accent.

"I've seen them in action," Grant said quietly. "I was surprised when I first witnessed it as well." He watched the wraiths until they broke off into several groups and dispersed to their assigned areas.

Once the wraiths were gone, Grant gestured to the group of men to come in closer. Even though he was anxious to join the search, he wanted to meet up with each one of the Keepers in attendance. He moved about the group, greeting many of those that he had known for a long time and meeting some for the first time. He was glad to reconnect face to face with many of the Keepers he hadn't seen in a long time, but his ulterior motive was to see if anyone present had a gold tooth that was visible when he talked.

After making the rounds and not finding anyone with a gold tooth, he had them bring the map of London out for another look. Once he found out from each Keeper which area they were going to search, he marked it on the map. Once all the areas were covered, the Keepers dispersed to their assigned areas.

"We'll keep in touch through our mobile phones," the local Keeper with the British accent stated before they broke up and scattered.

"And wraith messengers!" the Keeper with the cockney accent added. His exuberant voice sounded like he relished the action and the hunt.

Soon everyone was gone except Weldon and Grant. "What do we do?" Weldon asked.

Grant stared at the London skyline as he thought. "Show me her last known location," he said as he decided where he wanted to start.

"I've been there," Weldon stated, "and the police have been there. There are no clues. She simply vanished."

Grant sighed heavily as he turned to place his hands on the elder gent's shoulders. He bent down slightly to look him in the eyes, "Please," he whispered, "I need to do this."

Weldon studied him solemnly for a few minutes, then nodded.

"Thank you," Grant whispered.

CHAPTER FIVE

After a taxicab ride through the maze of London streets, they both got out to stand on a street corner. Weldon paid the cabbie and sent him on his way while Grant turned slowly, noting the crowd of buildings on each of the streets leading up to the intersection.

"This is where the police said her phone GPS went dark," Weldon muttered hopelessly as he moved to Grant's side.

Grant was silent as he continued to intently study the buildings, street, and people. During his survey, he wished he could somehow link with Charlotte telepathically or that there was some way that he could be drawn to her. His wishful musing was interrupted when he saw a group of wraiths fly by and through a building. He was sure it was led by Becker.

Weldon had seen them, too. "At least they are trying," he muttered softly as his face creased with sadness.

Grant turned to the older man to awkwardly place an arm around Weldon's grief-stooped shoulders and give a brotherly squeeze. "We will find her," he said confidently. *We have to have hope,* he thought as he worked to convince himself to find that hope somewhere, somehow.

Weldon's cell rang. He took it out of his pocket and looked at the display. "Of all times," he muttered darkly.

Grant looked at him curiously.

"Yes," Weldon answered the phone. He nodded his head as he listened. Soon his irritation became intensified interest, then flared into anger. "Let me talk to the nurse," he snapped.

Grant could see Weldon's fingers tighten on the phone as he held it away from his ear. Even though it was not set on speaker, he could hear a whiny voice talking fast and loudly.

"Do not argue with me, Curtis," Weldon snapped into the phone.

Grant's eyebrows shot up in surprise when he heard who had called.

"I know where you are. You cannot contact anyone without an attendant or nurse with you," Weldon continued, his voice dropping to a low growl.

Grant heard the voice on the phone get even louder. He still couldn't make out the words, but he could hear the maniacal tenor to them. He shook his head and was going to politely phase out the rest of the one-sided conversation until there was a sudden silence. Weldon placed the cell against his ear again. Soon he looked relieved and started to talk again, sounding more like himself.

"Yes, thank you," he paused as he nodded. "That is quite all right." Another pause. "Jerry, I need to know, was anyone in contact with Curtis? Did he get a phone call or did someone visit?"

Grant saw Weldon's lips set in a grim line as he got his answer. Weldon looked up at Grant and nodded. He wanted to ask questions immediately but forced himself to wait as Weldon listened and nodded.

"Thank you, Jerry." Weldon said. "Please put on his records that no one is to visit him or call him except for me or his sister, Charlotte." He nodded again. "Oh, and if his sister calls, can you let me know immediately?" He nodded again.

"Thank you. And you say the doctor will be there soon to sedate him?" Another nod. "Very good. Thank you for your help."

Grant couldn't wait any longer. "What happened?"

Weldon was in no hurry to answer the question. He slowly replaced his phone in his pocket as his face reflected deep thought. After a few minutes, he looked up at Grant. "We have been advised by Curtis to call off the search for Charlotte or she will die."

Although the words were spoken softly, the message hit Grant like a punch to the gut. After the shock cleared, his anger started to build. He was about to open his mouth when Weldon raised a hand.

"I suggest we go over there," he nodded toward the other side of the busy intersection. Grant was amazed by how calmly Weldon was now acting. It was as if the call galvanized his fear and worry into an intense resolve.

Grant looked over to where the older man had indicated to see a pub and a nearby tea shop. He glanced over at Weldon. "So what is it? Biscuits or booze?"

"A good English tea can calm the spirit and heighten the mind," Weldon answered sagely as he headed for the tea shop.

Grant hesitated as he looked at the pub. He was never much of a drinker, but the way he felt at the moment, he could change his mind. Instead, he listened to the wise words of his friend and followed him to the tea shop.

After they settled at a table and were served fragrant, fresh-baked scones and a pot of steaming Earl Grey tea, Weldon started to tell him more details. "Jerry, that's the attendant on duty, said Curtis was visited by a man with dark hair and eyes. He was tall and slender and spoke with a slightly foreign accent. He had told them he was a family friend. When they asked Curtis, he readily agreed," Weldon said as he stirred his tea. Soon he stopped and slowly put the spoon down. "I hadn't thought to put restrictions on his visitors."

Grant shrugged as he bit into a light, flaky scone and chased it with tea. He was worried sick about the situation but hadn't eaten since a light meal on the plane several hours ago. He needed at least a little something to keep him going. After he swallowed, he asked, "Don't they make visitors sign in and out?"

Weldon nodded. "They do. However, when they checked the log, they found a blank space where the signature should have been."

"Seriously?! What did he use? Disappearing ink?" Grant shook his head. "I wonder if the name would have been false anyway."

It was Weldon's turn to shrug. "Hard to know now." He moved his scone on the plate but didn't take a bite. "You think it was our evil Keeper?"

"Could be," Grant agreed. He had already been thinking along those lines. "If so, we have more of a description."

Weldon nodded. "Anyway, this morning Curtis got a call. After that he demanded to talk to me. He claims to know where Charlotte is. He was given the warning to pass to us. And he wants out to take us to her."

Grant pursed his lips as he looked out the window and thought. Somehow that seemed wrong to him. He met Weldon's eyes.

"I think he wanted to get out so he can escape," Weldon said as he seemed to read his thoughts.

"I think you are correct," Grant replied as he looked around the tea shop and then out the window. Suddenly, his eyes focused on the scenery outside and realized it was a perfect view of the corner that was the last known location of Charlotte.

Weldon saw him looking intently out the window. "The police questioned everyone here. No one saw anything."

"I'm sure that's true for any potential human witness." Grant turned from the street view until his eyes settled on the English wall clock that was on the wall opposite the window. "There's a wraith in there."

"Don't you think they would've come forward if they saw anything?" Weldon asked as he studied the clock.

"Saw what, luv?" The waitress came to check on them and heard the last of their conversation.

Grant looked up at her and smiled as he tried to be casual. "Oh, the woman that went missing from over there." He nodded toward the street.

The middle aged woman looked out the window to the corner indicated. At first, her forehead wrinkled in thought. Suddenly, she bit her lip anxiously. Grant and Weldon looked at each other. Something was obviously bothering the waitress.

"Is there something you remember?" Weldon asked softly.

"Aye, sir." She started wringing her apron between calloused, hard-working hands. "There be something. A small, blonde-haired lass?" she asked anxiously as she looked from Weldon to Grant.

Grant nodded his head slowly. When she looked to Weldon, Grant switched his attention to the clock. The wraith was stirring, and he sensed something wrong. He slipped his hand into his jacket pocket.

"Aye, sir." The woman was breaking out into a sweat as if she battled a strong mental enemy. "I seem to remember a beauty of a lass. She was fighting a tall man with dark hair."

Grant was not surprised when the wraith exploded out of the clock. He quickly removed his hand from his pocket to show the shadowy being what he held. He was quickly rewarded as the rampaging charge at the waitress was cut short. When Grant stretched his arm to wave the object nearer to the hovering wraith, the alien recoiled violently away as he stared hatefully at Grant.

Grant saw the wraith try to maneuver away from him and attack the woman from another direction. He tossed the cube to Weldon, who was watching the situation closely. He caught it neatly and also held it out to block the wraith from advancing. Grant quickly reached into his pocket again and pulled out another cube.

When the wraith saw that he couldn't get to the woman, he flowed through the window to the street. As he disappeared into a nearby building, Becker and her group came out of another one.

Grant shouted at her telepathically. She stopped and looked at him. He sent his memory of the wraith and where he went. She and her group turned as one to chase the being.

"Oh, that is a pretty thing," the waitress was looking at the dull, silver cube in Grant's hand.

"Ma'am," Grant gave it to her with a flourishing gesture. "It is yours."

"Oh, thank you, kind sir," she held it up, looking at it from every angle. "Oh, yes, I remember," she said as she turned the cube, having it reflect muted light from all its faces. "The gentleman, no, the rogue pulled her into a van." She hummed to herself as she thought awhile. "Yes, I do remember the tag." She took out her order pad and wrote down some figures. Tearing it off, she handed it to Weldon. "I hope you find the lass," she said, then tears came to her eyes. "Why did I not remember that?" She wiped a tear from her cheek. "I could've told the coppers…"

Grant stood and put a kind hand on her shoulder. "It is okay, ma'am. Sometimes things slip our minds. What's important is that you have remembered now."

"Yes, I guess." She slipped the cube into her pocket.

"Keep that cube with you," Weldon said as he stood. "It could help you remember things better."

"Thank you, sirs!" She smiled as she bobbed a curtsy. "I do hope you find the lass safe and soon!"

"As do we," Grant said as Weldon paid for their tea.

After they walked out of the shop, they stood on the curb.

"That's why the wraith didn't come forward," Grant muttered.

"It's one of the evil ones," Weldon concluded the thought.

"And under the guidance of the evil Keeper. It was posted there so that there would be no witnesses."

"Will she be okay?" Weldon asked as he thought about his granddaughter and worried about what she was going through.

"There would be no reason to harm her," Grant said as he looked toward the building the wraith had gone into. "I wonder when we will hear from Becker."

Weldon seemed to take what he said to heart. After taking a deep breath, he changed the subject. "How did you come by one of those cubes?" Weldon asked as they walked along the bustling street toward their hotel.

"I brought a few with me," Grant smiled to the older man. "I thought they might come in handy."

"How did you get them by customs and such?" Weldon asked curiously.

"Well." Grant rubbed his chin. "Becker kind of helped. She distracted the customs officials. All that was needed was a few moments."

"Ah," Weldon responded with a knowing look. "The wraith touch. Can be for help or harm."

"That's it," Grant smiled as they entered into the hotel.

CHAPTER SIX

Charlotte wasn't sure where she was. She felt distant. Her mind was foggy and unable to keep her thoughts together. When she opened her eyes, the room spun in and out of focus. The visual motion made her nauseous. Every sound was muffled and hollow. She felt that she was lying down on a bed, but that was all she could make out with her scrambled senses.

She could barely remember that she had left the hotel to get something but then was grabbed by a man with a gold tooth. *Gold tooth.* She focused on that thought. *Gold tooth,* she mentally repeated hazily. *What is so important about a gold tooth?* She thrashed about as she tried to find the memory.

Suddenly, she felt a presence. One she wanted to get away from but couldn't. She felt her arm grabbed and a sharp pinch. As she slipped into the murky depths of unconsciousness, she heard voices echo in her head.

"We can't keep her down like this."

"We will until they've stopped looking. They should have the message by now."

With her last bit of conscious thought, she shouted in her mind, *Becker!* Then she was out cold.

Becker was chasing the wraith on the other side of London. She had started to figure out they were on a wild goose chase when she heard Charlotte's cry. When she stopped suddenly in mid-air, the group of wraiths with her stopped and waited for orders. She had a general sense of direction about where the cry came from but not the exact location. She waited to see if any further communication would follow. After a minute, she informed her group and the rest of the wraiths in the area that Charlotte was still in London. Sending them the general location of her cry, they concentrated their efforts. Not wanting to get her Keeper's hopes up, she decided to wait to tell him anything until she knew something definite one way or another.

The wraith they had been chasing pulled up and stopped as he wondered what happened. He could see the group and sensed a message had been sent out by the leader. He wasn't sure what it could mean so he returned to his Keeper. Becker saw him moving off and signaled a member of her team to secretly follow him.

Soon the evil wraith whisked into the room where his Keeper was working at his desk. He relayed the news of what happened.

"You fool!" the Keeper shouted as his dark face turned darker. He jumped out of his chair to storm off to find his helper.

He found the other man anxiously checking the unconscious woman. He looked up at the Keeper with an expression of worry and pain on his face. "I told you we shouldn't have given her so much." He was surprised when a fist was driven into his face.

"It wasn't enough!" the other screamed at him. "They heard her!" He stalked around the room as he peered around the curtains in the windows to see outside. When he pulled back from the window, he fretfully glanced around at the ceiling and walls. "They will find us soon."

The other man held a hand to his bleeding nose as he checked his teeth with his tongue. He didn't dare speak. He knew that if he gave any suggestions, even helpful ones, he would be rewarded with another punch.

The evil Keeper stopped suddenly and snapped his fingers. "Ah, the sewer."

He grabbed the limp woman and threw her over his shoulder. When the other man didn't follow, he turned and glared at him. "You had better come. If they find me, they will know how you helped me." He stormed out of the room.

The other man, his nose still bloody, grabbed his bag of drugs and followed.

Thirty minutes later, Weldon and Grant, along with several wraiths, burst into the flat where Charlotte had been.

"Right place, wrong time," Grant muttered as he looked around the small living space that was made up as a small reception area for an office. He walked through a nearby doorway and found an unmade bed. Peeking out from under the wadded-up blankets, he saw something that looked familiar. He pulled it out and saw it was one of Charlotte's sweaters. Holding it close, he smelled her fragrance and almost cried. Instead, as he gripped the fabric in clenched fists, he let it fuel his anger and determination.

He walked out of the bedroom and handed the sweater to Weldon, who was in the middle of the reception area, looking around sadly. "We were too late," Weldon moaned as he hugged his granddaughter's sweater.

Grant gave him a one-armed hug for a moment, unable to say anything to comfort the older man. Moving off, he explored the rest of the flat to search the place for clues.

There wasn't much more to this small flat besides the living area, the bedroom, and an office. In the office space, he found a desk with its surface strewn with documents. He knew Weldon had followed him, so he didn't look up as he sifted through the papers to find a name. "It looks as if he left in a hurry," he muttered as he noted that many of the forms were partially filled out. He started reading the papers. "These are documents from an importer/exporter," he pointed out, holding out pages for Weldon to take a look at them.

"I have heard of this outfit," Weldon said as he glanced at them. "I've never used them. Their practices were known to be disreputable."

"Makes sense," Grant muttered darkly. "If our evil Keeper is the head of this operation, it wouldn't likely be aboveboard."

"True," Weldon answered. "Good and bad water doesn't come from the same faucet or stream."

"Very well put," Grant stated as he pulled a desk drawer open and found business cards. "Ah, here's a name." He waved one of the cards. "Max Headroom." He stared at it after he read it. "Sounds made up."

Weldon grumbled something as he looked through a cabinet that had been locked until he forced it open. After rummaging around in each of the deep drawers, he reported, "I found names."

"Names?" Grant turned from the desk to look across the room at him.

Weldon pulled a fistful of passports out of a file drawer. "Names," he repeated as he walked over to the desk to drop them on top of the paperwork.

"I count fifteen passports," Grant noted as he spread the pile apart so that each one of them could be seen.

"So do I," Weldon confirmed as he picked each one up and looked through them. "Several are U.S., some are British, German, and French."

Grant also looked through them as Weldon set them down. "They all have different names, and none of them match the business card." He glanced at each of the photos, noting the vastly different appearance of each alias with a change in hair style, expression, clothes, facial hair, and glasses with various frame styles. Going back through them to closely compare them, he tried to mentally compile an idea of what the evil Keeper should look like. The only common denominators were dark hair, dark eyes, and light brown skin. "I guess we can get a general idea of what he looks like," he commented as he put the last passport down; then he looked around. "I wonder. I find it strange that he didn't care about leaving all this."

Weldon pulled out his phone and took pictures of the passports and names. "I'm contacting the PI I have used before. I'll get them on this and see what they can find out. I'll send them the license plate number from the waitress as well."

Grant nodded and then asked, "What about the American Embassy? Have you contacted them yet?"

Weldon looked up at him. "I will, if none of our resources get her back soon." He nodded toward the wraiths that were searching throughout all of the rooms. "I doubt the government has anyone as efficient as they are."

Grant watched the wraiths for a while as well. He had to agree with the assessment. "What are they looking for?" he muttered more to himself than Weldon as he noted the circling pattern of Becker's team. They were obviously looking for something.

Weldon looked up from his phone, pausing from his communication with the security firm. "Their own clues?" he ventured. "You know them better than I do." He started tapping the phone again as he finished his message.

"Well," Grant stated as he picked up a nearby briefcase to shove all the passports and papers in, "I hope they have something to follow."

As he picked up the case to gently shake it to settle the contents, he noticed several wraiths gather around, staring at it. After a few moments, he saw Becker come through the group and start to inspect it closely. She hovered so close as to almost get in the main compartment.

Grant was puzzled. He had never seen this type of attentive interest in an object from the wraith. "Becker?" he asked quietly. "What is it?"

Weldon saw what was going on and came closer for a better view. He met Grant's questioning look and shrugged.

Becker finished her inspection and hovered in front of Grant. He received a mental image of some sort of device that was hidden in the briefcase.

Grant dumped everything out of the case onto the desk again, not caring that part of the contents slid off the table onto the floor. He started to look over the main compartment and pockets. When he didn't find anything, he closely inspected the walls. He felt a slight thickening in one section and felt sure he had found the device. Pulling out his pocket knife, he carefully split the seam and used two fingers to extract the object.

Weldon bent forward to view it closer. "A microphone?"

Grant shook his head as he turned the wafer- thin, black device to study it. "I believe it's a tracker." He closed his eyes and sighed. "Mind tricks," he muttered. He threw the device back into the open case. "He knew we'd be interested in all this and would need something to carry it in. In fact, it was very convenient." He looked around the office again. "He would have had to plan for this…"

Weldon looked around as well. "I bet this place is bugged," he whispered.

"I am certain of it," Grant said, not bothering to lower his voice. The evil Keeper would know the game was up by now. "There's nothing more here that will help," he concluded briskly. "Everything here is a plant."

Weldon looked around and nodded. "Let's go."

They left everything they found there, except Charlotte's sweater. When they got out of the building, Grant had Becker check out the loosely woven, light brown sweater. She didn't find anything suspicious. "So, it was simply left behind?" he asked her. She nodded sadly as she met his eyes. He gently folded it over his arm, determined to have it ready for her when they found her.

Weldon had hailed a taxi and stood by it, waiting for Grant. Before they got into the cab, Grant looked up at Becker hovering over them with her team. He asked, "Are they on their way?"

She nodded tightly before she sped away.

When they got settled into the taxi and the driver pulled away from the curb, Weldon leaned over to quietly ask, "What was that about?"

"The wraiths can follow the tracker beacon back to the scanner," Grant said quietly, not wanting the driver to hear him over the music coming from the front of the cab. "Although they don't like electronics, they are sensitive to certain wavelengths of sound waves. That was what the wraiths were so interested in back there. They were trying to pinpoint the device."

"Ah," Weldon's face brightened as his lips split into a grin. "He might have outfoxed himself."

"I am sure he has," Grant said as he smiled. He felt much better than he did earlier. His spark of hope grew a bit larger. "They will send word. She wants us to stay at the hotel. I think he may be able to track our phones."

CHAPTER SEVEN

Down in the sewer, the dark-haired man slammed down the scanner as his expression darkened in barely contained anger. He had heard that his tracker had been found through his eavesdropping device and almost threw it down along with the other. He had no idea that it was being traced back. He was angry because the device had been found.

He had wanted to know where the paperwork would go so he could intercept it or bribe whoever got their hands on it. He hadn't planned for all his aliases to be discovered. Since he didn't have time to clear out his office, all he could think of to do was to leave out the briefcase he gave to his couriers to haul his money. He hadn't counted on Weldon taking pictures of the passports. "For an old geezer, he sure knows how to use tech!" he grumbled out loud to no one in particular. He kicked the offending scanner against the wall as he stalked back to where they had laid Charlotte down.

They were on a narrow ledge down in the sewers beneath the city. He glanced at the sewage flowing by in an open trench between the ledges on either side. He tried not to breathe too deeply in the fouled air. He knew they couldn't stay there for long, but he was hoping that they could let the trail go cold for a bit. He was still unaware that even with the abuse, the scanner was still active and its signal was quickly being closed in on by a large group of wraiths.

"Carlos, we cannot keep her here," muttered his battered assistant, Dr. Malcolm Saunders. He was checking on the unconscious woman as he knelt by her. His concern for his patient was quickly overpowering his fear of the other man.

"What did you say?" The evil Keeper turned abruptly to glare at him. He didn't even glance at the woman he kidnapped to assess her condition. He didn't see that as she lay on the cold, damp concrete, even in her stuporous state, she was shivering with beads of cold sweat popping up on her face and body.

The doctor desperately tried to wrap his coat around her. His anger spiked as he stood to abruptly wheel around to face the other man. "You are endangering her life!" He pointed down at her. "You should've brought blankets or something!" He shoved his face into the other man's sneering face. "I thought you cared about her!"

Carlos put hands on hips and leaned forward as he thrust his chin out. The other man stepped back a pace. "I do care about her. You were there, Malcolm. You heard where I was taking her. You could've brought blankets and everything she needed." He straightened up and abruptly turned on his heels. "If she dies, it's on you!" he shouted back over his shoulder as he stormed up the sewer until he was out of sight.

The doctor held his breath as he listened to the echoes of sounds coming to him from a distance down the sewer. He could make out the metallic twang of someone climbing up a metal ladder and the sharp rasping of metal on metal as a manhole opened, then again as it closed. When the last echoes died down, he let out a deep breath. "I couldn't hear where you were taking her," he muttered angrily. "My ears were ringing, thanks to you!"

He thought about punching the nearby stony wall, then changed his mind. He was a surgeon; he needed his hands. Instead, he kicked it. Pain shot up through his foot into his leg. *I hope I didn't break a toe,* he thought miserably as he hobbled back over to the woman. He tucked her close into the wall, hoping to keep her from rolling off into the nasty water that flowed by them. After snuggling his coat around her, he slid down the wall to sit by her. As time went by, he periodically checked her pulse and felt her cold, clammy forehead.

Malcolm sat staring down the dark, dank tunnels waiting for his cruel master to return. Periodically, he looked down at the ground as he shook his head. Inwardly, he seethed with anger to cover the shame that landed him in this predicament. He checked the unconscious woman again. He knew he was in more trouble than he was before. *How did Carlos find out about my secret?* he asked himself miserably and not for the first time. It was one that was dark and dirty enough to leverage him to be forced to help in this kidnapping.

As he sat in the damp, cold stench, his mind started to clear. He looked around and wondered where his blackmailer was. He looked at his watch; it had been over an hour since he had run off down the sewer. He began to wonder why he was waiting…

* * * * * * *

Becker stopped the troops that were with her. They were ready to swarm the man they had just found with their Keeper. She was angry and wanted to hurt him as much as they did, but something about his actions made her stop and watch.

She saw the man look down the tunnels and check his watch. She noted Charlotte on the ground wrapped in the man's coat. She thought she knew how this man fit into the situation when he squatted down and checked on Charlotte with worry on his face and written in his action.

She instructed the others to secure the perimeter. She was surprised the evil Keeper hadn't left some of his wraiths to guard them. She figured he would correct his mistake soon and wanted to be ready for them.

Her suspicions about the man with the Chosen One were fully confirmed when the man snapped out of his thoughts and started to move.

* * * * * * *

Malcolm had had enough. His decision to take action was swift and urgent. Hoping he hadn't waited too long, he gently scooped up Charlotte and walked as fast as he could down the ledge to find an exit in the opposite direction he had seen his blackmailer go.

Malcolm wasn't sure how he was going to get her out by himself but he was determined to try. He had decided that it would be stupid to wait for his tormentor and risk an innocent woman's life. He was going to get her help.

As he reached a metal ladder ascending to the street level, he laid Charlotte down as gently as he could. He stood catching his breath as he peered into the dark tunnel in both directions. He wasn't aware he had been followed by a group of wraiths. He never saw as one of the evil Keeper's wraiths appeared to attack him. The smoky being was quickly surrounded and restrained by Becker's team.

The man took out his mobile and held it up, trying to get a signal. He paced angrily when he couldn't get one. He stopped to check on Charlotte, then gently jostled her to see her reaction. She didn't react. He resumed his frantic search for a signal as he paced on the narrow ledge near her. While he held his mobile in the air, he stared at the screen as he tugged at his hair with his other hand. He was obviously torn about how to proceed.

* * * * * * *

Becker had already sent one of her team to find the nearest Keeper. She had also tried to contact Grant but had trouble reaching him. Arriving too late at the last place Charlotte had been had affected him deeply. As he had waited at the hotel for word, he had slipped into a state of mind clouded with high levels of fear and worry that prevented her from being able to connect telepathically with him.

She was distracted from her efforts when she heard a shout from deep within the tunnels. The man with Charlotte stopped pacing and stood stiff after he had turned toward the sound. He was rigid with fear as his face blanched and glistened with cold sweat.

Becker looked down into the sewer and saw a mob of enemy wraiths pouring toward them. She called for reinforcements and assembled her group to face the charge. When she saw a man running down the ledge toward them, she knew instantly it was the one who had kidnapped Charlotte, the evil Keeper.

His face was red with anger as he ran furiously toward the man. He was so intent on punishing the doctor that he didn't notice the other wraiths.

"You fool!" he yelled. "Why are you close to a manhole?!" As he raced nearer, he drew back an arm, ready to punch him again.

Malcolm snapped out of his fear as rage took over. "I will no longer risk this woman's life for whatever scheme you are up to," he said coldly through clenched teeth.

The evil Keeper punched at him. The doctor was ready this time and blocked it. He delivered a punch into the evil Keeper's gut, causing him to double over and gasp for breath.

"She is going to the hospital," Malcolm shouted at the apparently incapacitated man. Dropping his guard, he spun on his heels to return to Charlotte to check on her. Carlos quickly recovered to tackle him. The force of the hit caused their feet to slip on the damp surface of the stone ledge and tumbled them headlong into the foul water.

Overhead, the wraiths from both groups had had a staredown as they sized each other up. The bad wraiths had been surprised to see a group of their enemy with their hostage. Suddenly, they flew at each other with screams of battle and were fully engaged when the bad wraiths saw that their master had been swept away in the sewage. Some stayed to fight, but most attempted to flee from the area. Becker had her team split up, some to overpower the remaining ones and the others to chase down the ones that fled.

Once the battle was over, Becker checked on Charlotte. Scanning her closely, she instantly felt fear for her friend's well-being. She sensed that the woman was on the verge of death and needed help quickly. As she let the others deal with the renegades, she sent an urgent message to Grant. Amplified by her fear, he heard it.

* * * * * * *

Grant was in his hotel room, mulling over his coffee. He was worried, and his mind played out scenario after dreadful scenario. He thought he would have heard from Becker sooner rather than later. The more time that went by, the more his impatience morphed into an air of defeat. Soon he abandoned the thought that the tracker signal helped. "He could've deactivated it," he muttered to himself darkly.

To add further weight to his worries, none of the Keepers had had any messages from their wraiths nor had found anything after all the intense searching. In frustration, he banged a fist on the table. With the sharp pain of the impact bringing him to his senses, he was glad he had been alone so there were no witnesses to see him lose his cool.

If we had only been faster, we would've caught them at the flat, he thought grimly. He knew Weldon was even more upset; he felt that he had failed to protect his granddaughter. Once his thoughts turned to Weldon, he wondered where the older man had gone. He was about to call him when Becker's message came through and stopped him in his tracks.

She had sent a mental picture of Charlotte and then a map showing where they were. He replied to her, grabbed his coat, and dialed Weldon.

"They found her," he said as soon as Weldon answered.

"Where?" the old man answered quickly.

"In the sewers," Grant said. "Where are you?"

"In the lobby," he replied.

"Be there in a moment."

"I'll grab a taxi."

CHAPTER EIGHT

When Grant stepped through the elevators onto the ground floor, he saw Weldon was outside the front door talking with a middle-aged couple. As he watched, it became a very animated discussion. By the time he arrived by Weldon's side, the man was smiling and putting money into his pocket as he pulled his wife away from the waiting cab. Grant didn't bother asking what happened as he followed Weldon into the open vehicle.

Even after Grant gave the destination instructions and urged the driver to get there as quickly as possible, the cab driver hesitated for a moment as he looked toward the couple still standing by the hotel entrance. Grant and Weldon looked out the windows to see the man pull out the wad of cash and wave it at his angry wife. Seeing the money, her eyes grew wide with astonishment, and then a smile came to her lips as she grabbed a bunch of bills from her husband. The cabbie, seeing that his assigned fare had definitely relinquished their rights, called his dispatcher to send another cab as he shot his car out into traffic and wove around various vehicles like a madman.

Both Grant and Weldon held on tight as the cabbie followed their instructions to hurry to their destination. During the ride through London streets, Grant kept glancing at Weldon. When Weldon met his glance, he shrugged. "What can you say? We needed the cab more than they did. The guy was happy with the money." Grant gave him a sidelong smile, then turned to look out the window as his thoughts were overtaken by worry about what they were going to find. The image Becker had sent him of Charlotte had him fearing for her life. He purposely didn't tell her grandfather what he had seen, choosing instead to wait until they knew more.

When they got to the location, they were surprised to see a group gathered around an open manhole. The crowd of onlookers was made up of a variety of people from all walks of life. Unknown to most of them was an overhead storm cloud-like formation of wraiths.

An ambulance was already there, along with the police. Grant pushed his way through the crowd and caught a glimpse of an occupied gurney being loaded into the ambulance. Weldon sprinted to scramble on board as he explained to the EMTs that he was family.

For a split second, Grant saw Charlotte before the ambulance doors shut him out. Her pale, haggard face sharply imprinted on his mind in that instant, more so than viewing a mere image. Seeing her for himself drove home the dire condition she was in. He was horrified by the implications of whatever the evil Keeper had done to her to cause her to look so gaunt in such a short time.

Her eyes were open. Did she see me? he wondered as he thought there had been a spark of recognition in her eyes. *I hope she remembered I came for her.*

He turned to the attendant who had shut the door. "Where?" he managed to croak hoarsely through a tightened throat.

The EMT told him the name of the hospital as he ran to get into the cab of the ambulance. As soon as he was in his seat, the door slammed, and the ambulance sped off, leaving Grant in its wake. His shock was starting to wear off as his anger started to build. Before he turned to the crowd, he saw Becker speed after the ambulance. He knew she would take care of her. He also caught a glimpse of Grant, Weldon's wraith, speed by so fast he barely registered his passing. Grant couldn't suppress a random thought, *Yes, they can travel very fast.*

He knew he would be following them soon, but first he needed to get as much information as possible. He turned back to the crowd. He noticed some men in hardhats talking to the police. He stepped in closer to hear what they were saying.

"Officer," one of the men was saying, his voice desperate as his hands waved around. "I just found her! I had nothing to do with why she was there!" He looked at the crowd around him, their faces grim and angry. When Grant looked closer at the onlookers, he noticed that most of them were local Keepers that had converged on the area as word was passed around that Charlotte had been found.

"Honest!" the sanitation worker gulped. "I was going ahead of the work crew to see if there were any problems at this junction. When I went down below, I found her. I immediately called for help!"

When the desperate Samaritan turned to the policeman with his back to the crowd, the Keepers looked for the wraiths that had found her. When the wispy beings nodded that he was telling the truth, they dispersed. The remaining bystanders had nothing else to see and drifted off. Grant, seeing there was nothing else to be gained there, hailed a passing cab. He needed to be with Charlotte.

* * * * * * *

The wraiths still had business to wrap up. Since the Time Keeper's vaults were still not working, the ones guarding the captured enemy wraiths needed to turn them over to the closest Sentinel to imprison them. Big Ben was the closest tower clock that had a Sentinel. Since they knew it had been shut down for major renovations, he had moved elsewhere. They were tasked to find him.

After sending scouts to other tower clocks in the area, they quickly grew concerned when he wasn't located. They expanded their search until they had to give up and contact the nearest Sentinel in the magnificent, six-hundred-year-old, astronomical clock, the Orloj in Prague.

When they arrived at the unique mechanical masterpiece, the Sentinel came out to meet with them in front of the intricate dials that measured time by five different methods: Central European Time, Bohemian time, unequal hours, position of the sun in the zodiac, and sidereal. Unseen by the humans trying to figure out the complex but renowned features of the working ancient timepiece, the wraiths talked with the Sentinel as they asked if he knew where the London Sentinel had moved.

The massive wraith shrugged in response as he drew out his cage of lightening and shadows through the picturesque calendar dial showing the month, season, and day of each saint. While the clock struck the hour, he shook his head as he looked around warily. While tourists watched the parade of the twelve apostles at the top of the clock along with the lower animated figures that included the depiction of death as a skeleton striking the hour on a bell, the wraiths turned over their prisoners to the Sentinel.

After he had placed the bad boys in his cage, he pushed it back into the intricate clock mechanisms. Afterward, he floated up to the top of the building to look around with a worried expression. Before the wraiths left him to go back to London, the Czech Sentinel told them that he had tried to contact the London one and couldn't locate him.

Later, when Becker found out about the missing Sentinel, she feared what it could mean. She quickly dispersed the others with her to look for him while she stayed with Charlotte. As the hours went by and the reports relayed to her kept being negative, she grew more worried as a sense of great wrongness kept increasing.

She hovered over Charlotte, trying to contact her mind and not getting any response. Charlotte had barely been conscious when she had been brought to the hospital and had sunk quickly into a deep coma. Becker had to let someone know about the Sentinel, but not just any Keeper. None of the other Keepers could interact with the Sentinels, and she feared what would happen if word got out to the others about the missing one. She looked to Grant, hoping that maybe he could help by being her close companion. But she couldn't contact him since he was too distracted by Charlotte's situation to be reached. She turned to Weldon, thinking a family member could possibly help, but Charlotte's grandfather was in the same state of worry and fear.

As Becker's frustration mounted and a sense of growing urgency overwhelmed her, she needed someone in this close-knit group to listen to her. Again, she tried desperately to get Grant's attention, but he was closed off to her, as if he didn't want to be bothered by her. She pulled back as she realized this and felt deep hurt. This human, her Keeper, with whom she had shared an existence for centuries, was closed off to her in ways she had never experienced.

She looked from him to Charlotte. She knew a deep bonding had begun between these two humans that were important to her. She understood that it was natural but she still felt a twinge of jealousy. *Surely I can still be a part of both of their lives,* she thought before she turned back to the problem at hand.

Unnoticed, she hovered above them, seeking options. Her scouts were still coming up empty in their attempts to find the evil Keeper and the missing Sentinel. She didn't think those situations were independent problems. All she could think was that the evil one had somehow trapped the Sentinel and was shielding his presence somehow.

Once she decided she needed to consult an Oracle, she had to seek one out, the rarest of their kind. She had heard that they preferred street clocks, even though those timepieces of older make that continued to remain in original condition were becoming extremely rare as well. Concentrating deeply, she was able to locate one and was relieved that she was nearby. Without bothering to try to inform Grant, she sped to the location.

CHAPTER NINE

As Becker drew near to the four-faced street clock, she saw that the Oracle was awake and waiting for her. As they hovered alongside the elaborate, pedestal timepiece, Becker bowed her head at the slightly larger wraith. The other bowed a greeting in return. "You have finally come," she addressed Becker, her voice low and hollow sounding.

"I have," Becker answered and waited.

"What is it you seek?" The Oracle met her eyes and held them.

Becker knew the Oracle was aware of exactly what she needed, but the rules were always such that the Oracle would only answer what was asked. So the questions had to be carefully worded. "We have been besieged by evil."

The wraith nodded slowly as her face appeared sad. She waited for Becker to continue. This information the Oracle already knew.

"The Chosen One has been found," Becker added.

Another nod from the other wraith. She knew this as well. She didn't speak since a question hadn't been asked yet.

"A Sentinel is missing," Becker blurted out, expecting another knowing nod. She was disturbed to see that the Oracle looked surprised at the news. The dread she was feeling grew.

She watched as the Oracle concentrated. Her form undulated, becoming more transparent and wispy. She knew this was a byproduct of connecting with subspace to gain access to whatever special abilities they had been given; for the Oracle, it was to peer across time and space. When the larger wraith stopped and regained her form, she hovered with her head bowed. Becker ventured to ask, "Where is he?"

The Oracle looked up with blazing eyes of white power and met her eyes. "You are known to your Keeper as Becker. You are the leader of the royal guard."

Becker nodded and waited.

"The royal family has finally come to Earth and is gaining strength."

Becker nodded again. She had suspected the weak and dying wraiths that were now recovering in Winston's pocket watches were part of the ruling family of the previous Society.

"Beware. If they have been possessed or touched by evil, if even one has, they will rip this planet apart."

Becker was shocked. She floated uncertainly as she stared at the other wraith. An Oracle never shared unknown information without being specifically asked, unless the situation was dire.

"The Sentinel is in the evil Keeper's possession. He is in the great evil's possession." The Oracle was quiet for a moment, then started speaking again, her voice lower and more hollow. "He is held in a tower clock with no tower. He is imprisoned and weakened by a cage of metal." She paused again, then sighed heavily with sorrow. "Evil will succeed to turn or destroy the Sentinel if our paladin is not freed."

"It hasn't happened yet?" Becker asked quickly. She saw a first ray of light in an ever darkening situation.

"He has resolve, but he is weakening," the Oracle said quietly. "He is in an abandoned warehouse."

Becker could tell that the larger wraith was tiring; the blazing eyes dimmed.

"You and the Chosen One are to confront the evil Keeper and free the Sentinel."

Becker sadly shook her head. "I cannot reach her."

The Oracle's eyes suddenly reignited to blaze again. "You can. You must reveal yourself." She then turned to flow back into the street clock's mechanism.

Becker floated outside the street clock for a while. She was shocked by what the Oracle revealed and had to take some time to process the information that had been given to her. Once her mind had cleared, she contacted one of her team and sent her to take a message to those that guarded the pocket watches. She warned them to watch for the emergence of the newly arrived wraiths and be aware that they could be compromised. She didn't reveal to them who they were, for she feared they would be slow to act if one of them was possessed by evil.

She contacted the wraiths that were searching for the missing Sentinel and told them what the Oracle had said. Although it wasn't an exact location, it narrowed down the search.

Next, she thought of Charlotte. She knew what the Oracle had meant when she had told Becker to reveal herself. She thought of what would need to be done, dreading the power it would take and the pain she would have to endure. She hoped she would survive the encounter.

In no time, she was hovering over the hospital bed. Grant and Weldon were still there with their heads down, each holding one of Charlotte's hands. She looked Charlotte over in hopes that she was showing signs that she was regaining consciousness but saw no indication. She was still in a deep coma.

Steeling herself, Becker dove into Charlotte's body, passing through flesh and bone, into her mind and thoughts, and reaching into her spirit and soul. Using her power, she grabbed the still, quiet core that was Charlotte and dragged her partially into a subspace pocket.

"Where am I?" Charlotte's voice reached out in confusion. Becker looked at the bright, wispy form she held. She smiled at Charlotte to reassure her.

Charlotte looked around to see an opulent, mother of pearl-like emptiness that vaguely glowed and shimmered in muted, swirling color. She was held by the hand of a bright creature that was stunningly beautiful. She noted her own form was wispy and light while the other had solid alabaster skin, deep gold eyes, and long golden hair that floated around her face. "Who are you?" she whispered in awe.

The other woman smiled reassuringly. "You know me as Becker."

"What!?" Charlotte was confused. The person standing before her was nothing like the wispy black being she had grown attached to. "I don't understand."

Becker shook her head and lifted her other hand to quiet her. She strained to keep holding on to her with one hand against the forces that were constantly pulling to draw Charlotte back into her own existence. "I don't have time to explain everything. This takes a lot of energy. I needed to talk to you and see if I could bring you back to consciousness."

"But," Charlotte looked around. "Where is this? Why can I hear your voice?"

"You are in a subspace bubble," Becker said quickly. She grew desperate as she weakened and the pain grew, but she knew she had to answer some of her friend's questions. "We are beings that exist in more than one plane of existence. The forms you see on your plane are our minds. I have pulled you into a place between existences so I can talk to you because of your coma state. It is important we talk sooner rather than later."

Charlotte still was overwhelmed but nodded to her. "Would you have told me these things?"

"Eventually." Becker smiled, then flinched involuntarily as knife-like pain tore through her being.

"What's wrong?" Charlotte asked in sharp concern as she studied her with worry.

"This is a painful process," Becker answered briskly, the pain making her voice sharp and crisp. "We were not created to be all together in one place. Plus the forces pulling you back are fierce to fight against."

"What do you need?" Charlotte asked urgently as she quickly shifted her focus from her curiosity to her friend's plight. She had many more questions to ask but realized there was an extremely short time limit to this encounter.

"The Sentinel that was in Big Ben is missing. He is trapped by the evil Keeper and is going to be possessed or destroyed by evil if we cannot stop it."

"What can I do?" Charlotte asked, greatly concerned.

"I need you to hold on to me. As we return to your plane of existence, I am going to pull you back into consciousness. It is likely going to be painful. I hope we survive the process," she added quietly with a deep feeling of concern. She violently winced as another electric shock of pain tore through her. The pains were becoming greater in intensity.

Charlotte hugged her friend tightly, then released her to hold both of her hands. "Let's go." Becker saw her close her eyes as she felt her tighten her grip on her hands.

"Okay." Becker steeled herself. "Hold on and don't give in to the pain," she warned. She closed her eyes and let herself be flung out of subspace. As her being split into parts across the planes of existences, her mind and thoughts firmly held onto Charlotte. As soon as she passed through the plane of human thoughts, she let Charlotte go as she prayed to the Power Above All that she timed it correctly.

She rematerialized in the hospital room above Charlotte's bed. As soon as she could shake off the last shocks of pain and the profound weakness from the transition, she looked down to see Charlotte moving her head and opening her eyes. As she hovered, she sagged in relief that the risk she took was rewarded with success. She smiled as Charlotte looked around without moving her head, then stopped when she saw her.

Charlotte's blue eyes momentary looked confused as she studied the black shadowy form that hovered above her. It looked as though she was going to say something, but then she smiled. The confusion was gone.

Even with that momentary reaction she saw, Becker wasn't sure if Charlotte remembered anything from her subspace experience. Before she could confirm anything, Grant noticed her eyes were opened. He nudged Weldon, and both stood up to lean over her.

"Look, she's trying to say something," Grant said excitedly.

Becker could hear Charlotte's very weak voice. Her words revealed that she remembered some of what she had seen. She watched the Keepers, wondering if they would understand what had been said.

"What is she saying?" Weldon asked.

Grant leaned close, placing his ear by her mouth. He listened for a while as she repeated something. Soon he stood up, his expression confused.

"What is she saying?" Weldon repeated as he saw that she had quit speaking and had a secretive smile on her lips.

Grant looked at him and then Becker. "She said, 'Beautiful Becker so white and bright. Needs you to find Big Ben's resident in the grip of night.'" He looked back at the older man to meet his questioning eyes. He shrugged in response.

Before the two men looked at her again, Becker slapped her forehead in frustration. When Charlotte repeated the message, she had managed to change it to a rhyme. She knew this would keep her words in the Keepers' memory longer and eventually would lead to further curiosity. She wasn't sure if the humans were ready to hear more about her race.

She thought no further about these worries as Grant and Weldon looked at her. She now had their full attention and was able to communicate with them directly to inform them of what she knew of the plight of the Sentinel.

In response to the message, Grant grabbed his cell phone and called several Keepers that he knew well. He asked them that while they were searching the area looking for the evil Keeper, to keep an eye out for an active tower clockworks in a warehouse. He didn't explain why but instructed them to let him know if they found one. With that done, Grant turned his attention to Charlotte.

Weldon continued to study Becker. "White and bright," he whispered to her. "So, more mysteries of your kind?" he asked quietly. "Or hallucinations from a mind full of drugs and sickness?"

Becker shrugged her shoulders and smiled. Inwardly, she worried about this human who she knew was very observant and inquisitive. She liked the older man, but she wasn't ready to have her people's secrets totally revealed. She was relieved when he looked away to check on his granddaughter when he didn't get an answer.

She checked on Charlotte again and saw that she had dropped into a natural sleep. She sensed that she was out of danger and communicated it to Grant, who was watching her intently. Seeing that everything was moving forward for the time being, she left to join the search.

As she sped out of the room, she caught Grant's mental message to her. "Let me know when you find the bastard who kidnapped her and did this to her." Before she slipped through the molecular construct of the wall, she turned to nod at him, acknowledging that she got his message.

CHAPTER TEN

Carlos sat at his desk, drumming the surface with a fist. Not only was he angry that he had lost her again, but he was also fuming because he had had to keep her sedated and was unable to woo the Ultimate Time Keeper to his cause. He frowned as he looked around at the mess produced from the search the Time Keepers had done at his office front. "All that, and I have to deal with this, too," he muttered darkly.

He had slipped in the back way, knowing that this place, one of his business locations, was being watched. He was certain they still didn't know who he was or have any idea what he looked like. He wondered if his former friend Dr. Malcolm Saunders would take the risk to go to the police. He shook his head, as he thought that was unlikely. His unwilling partner in crime had too much to lose.

His anger surged with the thought that it was because of the doctor that he had to swim up the sewers of London! He shuddered at the memory of the gagging stench he had been covered in until he could make his way to his personal flat to get cleaned up. He pushed that experience out of his thoughts as he focused his attention on what may have been taken from his office.

He glanced around at the paperwork and passports strewn all over the desk and on the floor that revealed his aliases. He knew from his eavesdropping that the old man had taken pictures of something. He glanced at the open briefcase lying abandoned on the desk. The only thing in it was the tracker, where it had been tossed back in after its discovery. He couldn't tell if anything had been taken. Most of it was bogus, so he didn't think anyone would be able to piece together enough to blow his cover. *But,* he thought fretfully, *there may have been something small that may have given them a clue to who I am.* He chewed a knuckle for a moment as he contemplated whether or not his secret identity would be revealed.

He rapped the desk once more with his fist as he stood up. He couldn't waste any more time worrying. Nothing he could do here. He needed to clean out and check on things at the warehouse. He scooped up all the documents and shoved them into the briefcase. After he forced it closed and locked it, he picked it up and was turning to leave when he stopped.

Something had grabbed his attention from the corner of his eye. He turned to look at it full on. It was the pocket watch he had stolen from the old man's mansion before the 'Day of the Wraith,' as he heard the Time Keepers call his failed attempt at world domination. With the days of desperation that followed his shattered plans, then the surge of excitement of hunting and capturing Charlotte, he had set it aside and only thought about it to keep it wound and running. It was hanging on a cobra-styled pocket watch holder placed on a shelf just in the shadows so it wouldn't be immediately noticed. The serpent's lower body slightly coiled to make up the base while its upper body and head were erect as if it was going to strike. The snout of the cobra's face was fashioned as a hook for the watch's hanger. He had felt that this was the perfect holder for the presence he had sensed brewing inside this particular watch.

He walked over to it, retrieved it from its hook, and held it. The presence he still felt within it seemed to be waiting as he hefted its solid weight. He had researched a bit about the timepiece and found that it was a French Oignon pocket watch made in 1680. He also learned that it was constructed of gilt metal, gold, and porcelain. He had recently attached a weighty gold chain with large flattened links, thinking of wearing the imposing pocket watch for show. As the links clinked softly as he handled the watch, he thought of how he had been impressed by whatever resided in the watch that it didn't want him to wear it and preferred to be left alone in shadowy seclusion.

At that moment, the pocket watch had his total attention. Something about it, like the first day he had stolen it, drew him in and forced him to narrow his entire focus on it. But he sensed that somehow the residing presence had changed. Involuntarily, his hand started to tremble as he held it. As he stared at the intricately carved, gilded face, he saw that the white patches of porcelain surrounding the numbers had started to flash dull green in a random fashion. Something powerful was emerging. As long as he had been a Keeper, he had never experienced this type of sensation before, not even when he dealt with the worst of the bad boys.

The tremor in his hand spread throughout his body until he shook so violently he dropped the pocket watch. The impact on the wooden floor shattered the watch's crystal. Carlos would've mourned the loss of the original glass but had no time to think about it. He was frozen in fear as his wide eyes stared in horror at what stood in front of him with the broken pocket watch at his feet.

A wraith had exploded out of the time piece at the moment the pocket watch had fallen out of Carlos' hand. He was a third again larger than the other wraiths, made up of the deepest black substance of shadows, and he was voraciously hungry. As his dark black, smoky face contemplated the human in front of him, he inched closer like a cat stalking its prey.

As the wraith closed in on Carlos, he frantically backpedaled to try to keep space between them. He not only felt the murderous hunger but also an aura of intense evil that infused the wraith's being. As panic fired up his muscles to run, he called out to his wraiths to come to his aide.

Within seconds, the wraiths that had been posted outside to stand guard came rushing in. Carlos expected them to attack the intruder but watched in surprised shock as they took one look at the newcomer and fled. Hot anger quickly replaced most of his fear and spurred him into action. He ran to the closet in his office and reached far into the back to retrieve a box. As he dragged the heavy box into the light from under a row of hanging coats, he tugged and sweated profusely as he kept looking over his shoulder at the wraith. The wraith appeared amused as he bided his time and watched the human scrabble around.

Ripping open the top of the box, Carlos dug in deep and pulled out fistfuls of dull grey cubes. After sweeping these into a pouch made up of his pulled up shirttails, he dug in for more until he had armfuls of them. When he turned to face the wraith, the dark smoky being drew back to study the cubes from a distance.

Carlos wasn't sure what to do, but he knew that to survive he had to kill this wraith. In desperation, he threw the cubes at the floor under the floating being until he managed to form a rough ring. When he was done, Carlos stepped back and watched. The wraith made a move toward him but was abruptly stopped by an invisible barrier.

At first the wraith was puzzled by the force that confined him. He thoughtfully probed at the cubes and tried to move them around. He quickly discovered that the cubes could not be touched without causing searing pain. Then he tried to melt through the floor but couldn't, and when he rose to find a way out over the top, he couldn't do that, either. As soon as he realized he was trapped, his reaction was explosive rage as the large wraith threw himself against the barrier time and time again. Every time he made contact with the invisible field, it hurt and made him rage even more.

Carlos backed further away as he watched fearfully. He wasn't sure how long the cubes could hold the berserker alien. With a sudden flash of inspiration, he snapped back into action to search around his office again. He knew he had a controller somewhere. As he frantically looked through the drawers of his filing cabinets and his desk, he kept looking back at the raging wraith. Sweat popped out over his entire body, making his hands slick while it poured into his eyes, causing him to blink rapidly.

Not much scared him, but this wraith terrified him.

His hand landed on a controller just as he felt something grab a hold of him. He struggled against invisible restraining bands to look back at the captured being. What he saw made him gulp heavily and whimper. The alien had settled into a deadly calm as he hovered in his prison and skewered him with blazing red eyes.

Suddenly, Carlos felt searing, hot pain as if he had been dumped into a vat of boiling oil. He tried to scream, but his voice was muted as his air was shut off as if he were in a pocket of vacuum. His adrenaline kicked in again to give him desperate strength to stave off passing out. With borrowed time, he painfully and laboriously moved his hand to point the controller at the wraith. Once it was aimed in the general direction, he fought to push the button as he felt his life being drained from him. With the last of his strength, he was able to depress the button enough to activate the device.

To Carlos' great relief, the alien started to violently shudder and then suddenly fragment. The resulting tiny wisps hung in midair within the confines of the enclosure. As he watched, the remnants of the powerful being slowly disintegrated into nothing. Once the power of the wraith was cut off, Carlos lay weakly on the floor as he drew in huge, gulping breaths. As his body cooled down, he stood unsteadily to face the lopsided ring of silver cubes and expected it to be empty.

He was bewildered when instead of an empty space, he saw a green-black cloud hovering where the wraith had been. He studied it closely and found nothing about it to fear. He felt sure that it was also confined inside the ring, as the wraith had been. Watching the cloud, he raised his hand to point the controller at it. He activated the device and expected the mysterious cloud to be destroyed. He was disappointed when nothing happened.

The cloud continued to expand and contract randomly as it hovered, and Carlos moved closer to study it. He called his wraiths back to see if they knew what this thing was. Hesitantly, they rejoined him, fearful of his reaction to their cowardly retreat when they saw one of their powerful royals but also of what else was going on. As they gathered to hover around the cloud in the invisible enclosure, they were also curious. Human and wraith studied the cloud. It seemed to be patiently waiting for something, or it was simply watching them; Carlos wasn't sure which.

Is it even alive? Carlos thought to himself. *It may be a cloud of residue from the destroyed wraith.* Plucking up his old confidence, he drew even closer. When he sensed a cold chill of evil, he was curious and interested as he wondered if this was some alien power he could use to gain world domination.

As he inched nearer and nothing threatening happened, Carlos' haughty attitude returned as he punched the air at the cloud. He was opening his mouth to jeer at it when, without warning, the miasma exploded. Wispy pieces of itself impacted and absorbed into the hovering wraiths and into Carlos.

The wraiths were instantly controlled by the entity. Carlos, however, fought and clawed at himself where the entity had entered his body. He grabbed at his throat as he coughed and gagged. After a few minutes of anguished struggle, he suddenly stood still and ramrod straight.

After a while, his mouth started moving in odd motions as his tongue flicked out and around. Garbled noises emitted from his throat. It wasn't long before the entity had a grasp of the human body. "Interesting," a hard voice grated through Carlos' vocal cords. "Very interesting." Then it moved Carlos' body like a marionette until, with practice, it could move smoothly.

With one mind controlling them, Carlos' body and the wraiths left the building. Carlos, trapped deep within himself, was appalled and fascinated by the sensation of not being in control of his own body. In his disembodied state, he wondered how the entity knew of the warehouse as it directed all it possessed to the old abandoned warehouse on the riverfront in Wandsworth.

Once they were in the large storage area of the warehouse, they faced a metal cage constructed in a cobblestoned fashion using dull, silver-grey cubes. Within its confines sat one of the smaller model tower clockworks that steadily ticked in its green metal frame. And within that was the Big Ben Sentinel who had found that he was trapped in the metal cage.

Even though Carlos was still trapped in his own body, he could see and sense the rage of the Sentinel directed at him and the evil wraiths that were guarding different sections of the warehouse. He also felt a strange satisfaction emanate from the piece of entity that possessed him.

Suddenly, the entity left all its hosts and reformed from its pieces into a dark green cloud. Carlos slumped to the floor for a few minutes as he needed time to regain control over his body. When he was able to stand up, he saw that the miasma hovered over the cage to probe and hound the Sentinel as it tried to find a way to take him over.

He looked away as his body started to shake, a delayed reaction to being unwillingly possessed. He knew he wasn't a nice person, but as his head cleared after the entity had left him, he was appalled by the level of evil he had been exposed to. He never had believed in evil possessing someone, but he didn't know how to describe how he felt before and after that dark green smoke had left him. He sincerely hoped it was all out of him and that it wouldn't return to imprison him in his own body again.

After watching the battle in the metal cage between the Sentinel and the evil entity for a while, Carlos had a strange compulsion to stay and see what would happen. He knew that he should be running from the strange miasma that had possessed him, but he had set up this trap for the Sentinel and had no intention of leaving it for someone else to control. As he thought more on the situation, he began to convince himself that the appearance of the entity was a good thing. If it could control the Sentinel, he could still have a chance to get it to do his bidding. *Maybe…*he thought to himself. *But I may still need the Ultimate Time Keeper.*

As he went to find a chair in one of the offices located at the front of the building, his mind turned back to Charlotte. He was still upset that he had lost her. He hoped that when the Sentinel was converted, he would be able to control it, but he was worried. He was counting on Charlotte's doing that. He placed the chair in the middle of the vast room to sit and watch the metal cage. His dark eyes grew misty as he thought of the lone woman Time Keeper. *Oh, if I could've talked to her properly,* he thought dreamily, *she would've seen the purity to my purpose. She would've been glad to help me. She might have fallen in love with me, and we could've been married for all time.*

He snapped out of his daydreaming when he heard the shrieking of wraiths. He sat up to look over at the tower clock mechanism. As he intently watched the black and dull green roiling mass in the metal cage, he sensed the torment the Sentinel was being subjected to as the green-black cloud intensified its attack and attempted to forcibly invade him. Carlos' only concern was how long it would take before he could go to the next stage of his plan. He had absolutely no pity for the tormented being.

After he yawned in boredom, he made himself busy while he continued to wait. While he went looking for a small table to place by his chair, he checked in with the wraiths who were keeping watch on the perimeter. He directed a few of them to spy on the other wraiths and Keepers. After sitting back down in the chair, he called to update the other people he had charmed into his network of deceit. They were not Keepers, but they had been part of the previous failed attempt to control the world.

Once he was assured that his network was safely in place and that they were all still loyal to him, he revealed the rest of his plan to them and reminded them that this was another chance to help him gain world power through the wraiths. He warned them that they needed to act instantly once they received his signal so that he could move to the next step. When he attempted to contact Curtis, he was blocked by some vague new regulation. Shrugging it off, he figured that the Chosen One's brother was of no use to him anyway. Completing all that, he sat back and thought of his next move. After a moment, he started to call hospitals. He was determined to find Charlotte. He still felt strongly that he needed her abilities for the plan of world domination to work.

CHAPTER ELEVEN

Charlotte awoke the next day, sensing she was not in her own bed. Before she fully opened her eyes, she was aware of a weight across her. She opened them to find Grant partially draped over her as if protecting her. He was holding one of her hands, having tucked it under his bewhiskered chin. It looked as if he had been leaning forward in a nearby chair watching her when he fell asleep and slumped into the position she found him. Even though her mind was fully clear, she couldn't remember anything and wondered why she was in a hospital room.

She started to panic as she frantically tried to gather any memories to explain where she was. Before she reached freak-out stage, she became aware of Grant's softly snoring and could feel his breathing as his head lay on her chest. She slowly reached over with her free hand to run her fingers through his dark, curly hair that had a touch of grey at the temples. Her panic started to subside with a sense of safeness as her thoughts quickly turned to the memories she could readily recall. With that start, she discovered she could recall more bit by bit.

She remembered their talk in his clock shop and his hurt expression when she wouldn't let him go with her. She could remember the places she and her grandfather had been as they toured through Europe and visited the major tower clocks. She could remember up to London but couldn't remember visiting Big Ben. *Had I already, but can't remember?* she wondered as she thought to herself. *Where am I now?* When she heard talking in the hallway, she heard strong British accents in all the voices and nodded. *In England, at least.* She smiled, then turned her attention to pondering Grant's presence.

She was glad he was with her. Even though she couldn't remember all the details of what had happened, she had a distinct sense that it was something bad and that he came to find her. She suddenly grew desperately tired. Pulling his hand from under his chin, she grasped it with both of hers to draw it to her lips. After she kissed each finger, she tucked it under her cheek as she continued to hold onto him while she fell asleep, feeling secure and safe.

Suddenly she felt rough hands grab her and gag her. She had been on the street. She was going to see something, and then she was tied up and blindfolded. She tried to fight. She tried to scream. She struggled against the painful grip of his hands. She heard voices, then felt a sharp stab in her arm, and then nothing.

Shaking and screaming, she jolted awake as a cold sweat poured from her. She continued to cry in great, heaving sobs as she struggled against the bonds of her dreams. As the intensity of her terror started to wane, she realized that she was held in the embrace of very strong, muscular arms. When she quit struggling, the arms loosened just enough to free a hand to tenderly brush her hair from her face. She opened her eyes to look into the worried, dark brown eyes of Grant.

She licked her dry, cracked lips before she tried to smile. Her mouth was parched, but she managed to croak out a few words. "Why is it we always meet when I'm in a horrible state?"

Grant quirked a small smile then held her close. She couldn't see his face but heard him whisper, "I'm just glad to see you are okay."

She answered by reaching around him and holding onto him as she buried her face into his chest. He responded by tightening his hold a bit more, snuggling her up to him securely. They remained that way as she drew comfort listening to his slow, strong heartbeat, he feeling comfort in the way she relaxed into him. Their shared wish of wanting the world to pass them by and leave them alone was shattered as they heard someone speak.

"Can you let her go long enough to see if she can eat?" a female voice of authority spoke and expected to be obeyed.

They both startled apart to look toward the door. A nurse stood in the open doorway. As she walked toward Charlotte, Grant moved to sit on the chair by the bed. She worked in silent efficiency as she recorded Charlotte's vitals. Once that was done, she pulled the hospital table around to position it over the bed. She made sure the position of the bed was comfortable for the patient, then went out into the hall and came back with a tray of covered dishes. She placed it in front of Charlotte. Making sure everything was situated to her satisfaction, the nurse left the room on cushioned soles.

Charlotte lifted the lids on the plates. "Doesn't look too bad," she commented as she pulled out her fork and started to eat. Grant sat back and watched as she ate well, even for hospital fare. She was almost done when the doctor came by to check on her.

"Good to see you alert and eating well," he commented. He checked a few things in her records, then stood back. "Looks as if you should be able to be discharged very soon." He consulted her chart again. When he looked up, he asked, "Can you remember anything from your ordeal?"

Charlotte thought awhile. She shook her head. "It's a blank."

He studied her, then nodded. "Would you like a referral to a counseling service?"

She considered it. "No, not at this time."

He handed her a card. "If your memories do resurface, I urge you to call them." He nodded at the card in her hand. "That includes nightmares."

She thought about how she had woken up screaming in Grant's arms. She knew she had had a nightmare but couldn't remember any of the details. *How can I talk about something I can't remember?* she thought to herself. She kept a poker face as she handed the card to Grant for safekeeping. "I will keep that in mind."

Soon after the doctor left, Weldon entered the hospital room carrying two bouquets of flowers and a fist full of strings attached to a huge bunch of multicolored balloons that floated overhead.

Grant stood to help him wrangle the balloons and flowers into the room. The brightly colored balloons distracted Charlotte from dwelling on the vague, dark feelings the nightmares had left in her thoughts.

"Here's yours," Weldon said as he handed Grant a bouquet of various types of flowers in an assortment of colors.

"Aw, you got him flowers," Charlotte quipped from the bed.

Grant looked sheepish as he handed her the flowers. "They are for you. I....I," he stammered.

"He didn't want to leave your side for a moment. That's why he's starting to look like a mountain man," Weldon interrupted. He handed her the other bouquet of flowers, a large bunch of red roses. "These are from me."

She sniffed both bunches appreciatively. "Thank you." She placed them on the bedside table. "Did you get all those balloons?"

Weldon tied the huge bunch of balloons to the foot of the bed. "No, these are from the local Keepers. They are glad you are doing better. And they are sorry this happened on their turf. They had no idea the evil Keeper was from around here." He stopped when he saw her shocked expression. He looked to Grant, who was shaking his head.

"She can't remember anything," Grant said as he reached over to hold Charlotte's clenched hand. She was pale and shaking slightly. He tried to get her attention, but she stared off as if she were looking through the wall at something only she could see.

After a few minutes, she started to look from her grandfather to Grant and back. "I can't remember a thing," she whispered tightly. "What do you know?"

Grant and Weldon took turns telling her what they knew. Where she had been held, where she had been found, and how they were sure it had been the evil Keeper. She nodded as she listened, taking in every word. When they were done, she thought for a while. "I still remember nothing."

"You had a nightmare," Grant started gently. "Do you remember anything from that?"

She looked thoughtful as she tried to fit what they had told her to the feeling of terror she woke up with. Nothing emerged. She shook her head.

"It may return in time," Grant said quietly.

"Maybe," she nodded as she squeezed his hand.

Weldon cleared his throat. "There is a surprise for you that may help cheer you up. They have been patiently waiting." Charlotte furrowed her brow as she wondered who 'they' were and was about to ask when he smiled as he looked up at the balloons. "Okay, guys! She's watching!"

Charlotte and Grant watched in amazement as wraiths poured out of the balloons to fly in intricate patterns like precision jet fighters. When they all had emerged, they formed a mysterious symbol which slowly morphed into a heart shape.

Charlotte wiped tears from her eyes. "That was so sweet."

"Too bad there wasn't music to that display," Grant observed.

Charlotte looked at him in surprise. "But, there was!"

Grant's face fell. He hadn't picked it up. He glanced over at Weldon, who shook his head and shrugged his shoulders. He hadn't heard anything, either.

She patted his hand. "I'm sorry you couldn't hear. It was very beautiful. Thank you," she spoke to the mass of wraiths that hovered near the ceiling. "That was very beautiful."

They seemed pleased as they bowed to her, then left the room in all directions.

Charlotte looked up at the bunch of balloons hovering above her bed as they gently turned with the air currents flowing through the room. "I will never look at balloons the same way again," she whispered as she smiled.

Grant was so happy to see her smile. The image flashed in his mind of how she looked when they had found her. It momentarily superimposed on her as she was now. His cold fury returned now that she was out of danger.

"Where's Becker?" Charlotte asked, bringing him back to the present.

"She's busy." He searched her face. "Do you remember warning us about the missing Sentinel?"

"There's a Sentinel missing?" she looked at them in complete surprise.

"Answers that question," Weldon said as he sat on the opposite side of the hospital bed from Grant.

Grant rubbed his chin as he thought. "Do you recall they are working on Big Ben?"

"Yes, I was trying to visit it to check on the Sentinel before they started the work. I was planning on seeing where he would be staying." Her face became worried. "How long have I been out?"

"Big Ben has been shut down."

"Where's the Sentinel?" she whispered tightly.

Grant and Weldon looked at each other. "He's the one missing."

"I feared that's what you were going to say," she said as she gripped the hospital blankets tightly in clenched fists. She concentrated on trying to contact the huge wraith to see if he was still in the area. "Oh, no!" she exclaimed then winced as a sharp pain shot though her mind. She dropped the blanket and held her head.

Both Weldon and Grant reacted. "What's wrong?' they cried with concern at the same time.

To Charlotte, their voices were far away, almost hidden in a roar of mental noise.

"Should we call a nurse for pain meds?" Weldon asked quietly.

Charlotte barely heard him. She shook her head. "It would put me to sleep." She held her head tighter. "I need to concentrate."

"What do you think is going on?' Grant asked softly.

She didn't speak for a while. He wasn't sure if she had heard him. Then she furrowed her brow in thought as she spoke quietly, "It's a mix. There was a time distortion." She tilted her head as if she listened to someone or something. "It is buried memories, half-remembered conversation along with waves of mental anguish." Suddenly, she dropped her hands and asked urgently, "Where are my clothes?"

Weldon was the first to react. "Why?"

Charlotte threw the covers back and tried to get out of bed. When she couldn't, she stopped and stared in amazement at all the wires and tubes attached to her body. She traced them to the medical devices crowded at the head of the hospital bed. "I have to leave. I can't figure this out here. I have to get closer." She started to fight with the medical tethers that impeded her progress.

"Closer to where? Or what?" Grant asked as he rushed to save the equipment she was pulling over in her struggles. Weldon jumped up to get her clothes.

"The Sentinel," she said brusquely as she ripped out the IV catheter and pulled off the EKG sensors. As she kept the hospital gown closed around her backside, she grabbed her clothes that Weldon had placed on the bed and swept into the bathroom to change.

Grant and Weldon stared at each other. Each silently questioned the other while they both wondered what was happening. Weldon was the first to move. "I better tell the hospital staff that we are leaving before someone comes rushing in when their remote monitors start to alarm."

Grant simply nodded as he waited for Charlotte. Telepathically, he sent a message to Becker that they were leaving the hospital.

Becker stopped talking to her scouts when she heard the message. She smiled and knew the situation would quickly improve with the Chosen One back in action and on the move.

CHAPTER TWELVE

Carlos Lopez was frustrated. He had called all the hospitals in the area and came up empty. He wondered whether she was somehow being hidden from him under another name or orders were in place not to give out any information about where she was. He didn't have anything else to do, so he sat back to watch the ongoing battle in the metal cage.

He had acclimated to the presence of the evil entity and no longer feared it. *At least as long as it is preoccupied with another victim*, he said to himself. He watched with sick fascination as the dull, green-black miasma tried to infiltrate and bond with the Sentinel that he had trapped.

He tore his eyes away to watch the wraiths that were in the room with him. They were nervous. He shook his head. *Cowards!* he thought as he mentally put himself above the creatures that he felt he owned and controlled. He went back to watch the roiling and seething of the green-black cloud inside the metal cage. It was a massive battle, but he could tell the Sentinel was weakening.

Suddenly, the Sentinel used the last of his strength and bashed himself against the barrier. The power of the impact was enough to loosen some of the cubes making up the cage. Much to his dismay, Carlos' reaction had been immediate and involuntary as he jumped out of his chair and stood behind it with nerves hot-wired in anticipation to run to the door. When his racing heart settled down to a normal rate, he noted that the wraiths were laughing at him.

Scowling at them, he sat back down as he pointedly ignored them. He purposefully leaned back, folded his arms across his chest, and watched.

When he saw something change in the metal cage, he forgot his he-man posturing as he sat forward with his arms on the table, amazed at what he saw. The Sentinel had suddenly broken apart. He could see the wraiths in individual forms as the dark green entity tried to overtake each one.

His initial reaction of curiosity to this new event turned to anger when he realized the implication. "No!" he shouted. "We need the Sentinel! We don't need more wraiths!" He pounded his fist on the table. Carlos didn't notice that the other wraiths had moved as far away as possible from him. If he had thought it was because of him, he would be greatly mistaken. They had figured out what that entity was and would not dare shout at it, and they didn't want to be around anyone who did.

The green-black miasma pulled back; whether it was a reaction to his outburst or because of the breaking up of the Sentinel, Carlos could not tell. He suddenly felt his fear of this thing return like a tsunami as he watched it warily.

Whatever the reason, it hovered over the cage; it seemed to be brooding. When the individual wraiths either could not or would not rebond, the cloud started to move away. When Carlos saw that it was moving in his general direction, he bolted out of his chair, overturning it in his haste. He began frantically backpedaling toward the door, not daring to turn his back on it as he desperately tried to keep it from touching him.

His futile efforts to keep it from possessing him were punctuated by his sharp cry, "No!" as it descended upon him, despite his arms thrown up to cover his head. His last clear thought as it overtook him was that it was bad enough to have a piece of that thing plaguing him; now he had the whole thing.

Walled off into the core of his own being by the overpowering evil, he was able to contemplate his predicament and be aware of what his body was being forced to do. He could hear the entity's thoughts as it detailed its diabolic plans to its captive in a horrifying mental shout that beat at his psyche to break him down further. Carlos knew he had always had a bad streak, more willing to break laws and rules than to keep them. But this thing was more dark and evil than he had ever dared to dream of being.

Once the evil being had complete control over Carlos, it looked around the room with a cruel sneer, twisting his mouth as it caused Carlos's eyes to glow a dull, sickly green. His body slouched and tightened with suppressed aggression as it walked to where the tower clock mechanism ticked rhythmically in its cage of silver cubes.

"I can wait." The Keeper's mouth moved, but the voice was gratingly harsh and bitingly cold. "But you will be made to do my bidding."

It turned from the cage and appraised the hovering wraiths. "Gather the troops," it growled as it ordered them. "I have special instructions."

The bad boys, as the Keepers would call those evil wraiths, cowered in fear in front of this human who had been their Keeper but now was possessed by the force they feared the most, an unrelenting, merciless power of pure evil.

As the possessed Carlos stared at the wraiths frozen in the room, it grew increasingly angry. "Go!" it shouted, and the wraiths fled to do its bidding.

Walking back to the overturned chair, it set it back up to sit in it. It pulled the table in front of itself to lean on while it steepled Carlos' fingers as it prepared to watch the tower clock mechanism. "My friend," the evil entity talked to the body it possessed. "You started things for me. But since you were not able to finish it, I will do it." It looked around the room and muttered, "Hmmm, another world to possess. Another species to subjugate." It smiled wickedly as it reached up to yank out the gold tooth with a vicious wrench. As the socket bled, painting its host's lips red with blood, it licked borrowed lips. "Sorry, my friend. But it was too identifiable. We must be more clandestine."

The entity made sure to channel all the pain from the tooth pulling into Carlos's awareness. Carlos writhed in his personal hell as the pain further intensified his torment. *Why, oh why, did I steal one of the pocket watches from that old man's house?* he mentally moaned. Belatedly, he had finally realized what he was dealing with.

Yes, he thought sadly, *the great evil that the wraiths had named in their prophecy has come, and it is now in me.*

CHAPTER THIRTEEN

Becker and her team were checking out the warehouses along the waterfront. She was about to order her team to start on another warehouse when she saw a group of terrified wraiths fly out of a nearby building. She instantly recognized that they were part of the enemy wraith faction that they were looking for. She was amazed that they had taken no heed to their presence and showed no indication that they were even looking where they were going.

She called back her team as they started to chase them. She knew they were confused by her orders, but she didn't explain as her attention was locked onto the warehouse they had come from. In it, she sensed a presence that she had not felt in centuries. She suppressed a shudder as she thought of the Oracle's words and saw new meaning. What she had interpreted as a great evil was the evil Keeper. Now she knew that the Oracle had spoken of the great evil that had destroyed their Society. It had found them, and it was in this warehouse. She feared, as it was as foretold, that it was with the tower clock mechanism that contained the missing Sentinel.

She slowly approached the building. Yes, she could sense the tower clock mechanism but not the Sentinel. She hovered in place, her thoughts confused. Was she on a wild goose chase? She resumed her slow approach as she forced herself to filter out the evil presence, which grew stronger as she drew nearer. She knew how this entity worked and blocked any thoughts that could give it inroads to affect her.

She was circling around to the back wall of the huge building when she sensed the location of the tower clock movement. Concentrating even further, she was able to pick up the faint cries of hundreds of wraiths.

As her team approached the building behind her, she signaled for them to wait as she slipped through the molecular construct of the wall. She eased her face out through the inner surface only enough to see what was beyond it. She saw the tower clock movement in a cage of metallic cubes. She frowned as she remembered being trapped by one of those cubes in her clock not too long ago.

She tried to contact the Sentinel. At first, the response she received confused her. But when she suddenly realized what the source of the faint cries signified, she recoiled backward out of the wall. Her sudden flight caused the waiting wraiths to hastily retreat even though they didn't have a clue to why their leader had emerged appearing very angry and grim.

The Sentinel has broken up instead of succumbing to the great evil, she thought to herself as many questions enveloped her. *Would they survive after being bonded for so long? Could they rebond? Could evil possess them and then force them to rebond?* She shook her head in frustration. She had no idea. She needed more information.

She wanted to get closer, but the source of the intense evil energy was sitting in the same room, watching the tower clock movement. When she eased back into the fabric of the wall, she recognized that the evil Keeper they had been searching for was there, but she knew that the heightened intense presence of evil he exuded was new. She grimly realized that the evil entity was able to possess humans just as it did her kind.

Suddenly, she was aware of the shift in attention from the human. He turned to search the area she was in, to pinpoint her location. Before he focused on her, she saw the blazing green, nonhuman eyes. She knew all she needed. She backed away before it could see her. She contacted the others of her team to leave the area as she put distance between herself and the building.

Becker soon realized that the entity in the Keeper had sensed her and her general location as a team of wraith bad boys converged on her and her team. After a brief, intense battle, they were able to escape and quickly lose them in a high-speed chase through and around the buildings of London.

After they were clear of the enemy, Becker called her team members together for a quick briefing and to issue orders. A few of them she sent back to remain hidden by the building to watch it and monitor the situation. The rest she sent back to the Keepers to try to explain what was happening.

Once her team members dispersed to carry out her orders, she went to find Charlotte and Grant. She had to inform them as soon as possible. As she flew through and around buildings, she thought about their adopted world and shuddered. She had not ever wanted this evil to come here. She feared for everyone, wraith and human alike.

CHAPTER FOURTEEN

Charlotte rubbed her forehead as the cab raced through the streets. She was sitting between Grant and Weldon, both men taking turns watching her in concern and sharing looks of bewilderment with each other.

When they had left the hospital, she was determined to try to find the Sentinel even though she had admitted that his whereabouts were too vague. Then Weldon had a call from Scotland Yard informing him that the kidnapper's accomplice had turned himself in and they had taken him into custody. With this new information, Charlotte had the cab change direction and head toward Scotland Yard.

"Very strange," she muttered with her eyes still closed and her head resting on the back of the seat. It was the first thing she had said since they had changed destinations.

"What is?" Weldon asked his granddaughter softly.

She turned her head and looked at him with one eye slightly open. "The dreams one has while in a coma."

"You remember them?" Grant asked in surprise. "I didn't think people usually did. Are they anything about what happened to you?"

"No." She shook her head slightly. "It's about something else. It's only bit and pieces," she said as she slowly moved her head to look at him full in the face as he sat on the other side of her. "But they're vivid. Maybe it was the drugs the doctors said the kidnappers used on me."

"Maybe." Weldon nodded, looking thoughtful.

Grant looked through the cab window. His thoughts were distracted as the mention of coma and dreams led him back to the kidnappers. "Why is it you want to talk to the man that gave you the drugs?" he asked.

He didn't notice that she hadn't answered him as his mind skipped back to the worries of where the evil Keeper was as well as the missing Sentinel. He felt that it was a step backward to talk to the man who had been part of the plot against Charlotte. When he finally noticed the silence, he was further mystified when he turned his head to look at her and saw a slow smile spread across her face. She had noticed him looking at her in confusion.

"Because he can tell us who the evil Keeper is. Hopefully, he can also give us more details about him." She rubbed her forehead again and closed her eyes. "And I believe he saved my life."

Weldon and Grant looked at each other in shocked surprise.

"How do you know that?" Grant asked, trying to keep the skepticism out of his voice. He wanted to be careful and not upset her.

"Oh, a little birdy told me some things," she muttered.

Grant sat back. "Oh, Becker."

"She told me how he was there when the wraiths found me. He was worried and distraught, and he had thought to keep me warm with his coat. She had also seen that it looked as if he had been in a fight."

"She 'told' you?" Grant asked. He always wondered about and was slightly jealous of the deeper link she had with the wraiths. She understood their communications much better than any other Keeper he ever knew, including himself.

"Well, pictures speak a thousand words. The mental image she gave me of myself looking like crap and lying in a sewer spoke volumes."

Both Grant and Weldon wanted to pull her into their arms at the same time. They stopped when they realized they would be playing tug of war with her.

When she felt both of them give in, she smiled and laughed. "Thank you, you two! I feel the love. Relax! I'll be okay." She lifted her head and opened her eyes as the cab stopped in front of the police station. "Or at least I will be when this is all over."

After sending the cab on its way, they entered the building. The officers were expecting them and had them quickly escorted into the bowels of the building. As they met with the inspector on the case, they were told that the suspect was in a room, ready to talk with them.

"His name is Dr. Malcolm Saunders," the inspector said as he took them to the interrogation room. "He turned himself in yesterday." He stopped in front of a door. "He's in there. Good thing he's cleaned up. When he came in, he smelt like a sewer!" he said as he smiled at them. "It was awful!"

"Thank you for letting us talk with him. And for cleaning him up!" Charlotte smiled brightly at him. "Does he know I will be talking to him?"

The inspector nodded. "Yes, marm." He looked over the group. "Who will be going in? I have already talked with him. However, I will be monitoring the conversation and will have a constable in there with you."

Charlotte turned to Grant and Weldon. "You two won't be." When they started to protest loudly, she stated firmly,

"A constable will be in there. I will be safe. I need him to feel safe so he will talk to me. If either of you are in there, you will terrify him if he sees what I see in your faces right now."

Grant and Weldon stepped back when they realized she spoke the truth. They knew that they had both built up a protective rage that neither could be sure he could control.

"Remember, he is the flunky, not the guy in charge." She put a hand on the doorknob. "Go to the observation room," she ordered as she opened the door and walked into the room.

The room she entered was small with a table and a few plastic chairs. The slender male prisoner was handcuffed to the table. He sat in one of the chairs on the side of the table facing the door. Charlotte couldn't see his face as he slumped over with his head in his hands. He was dressed in prison garb with unkempt auburn hair

When she moved to the chair to sit across the table from him, he looked up. She immediately took note of his haggard face sporting dark red stubble on a usually clean-shaven face. His hazel eyes full of sorrow and self-loathing followed her as she sat down. She was surprised to see tears forming in his eyes. She had guessed before that the person keeping her drugged was being used by the evil Keeper. Now, she knew she was right.

She smiled at him and reached across the table to touch his hand gently. "Thank you for trying to take care of me."

He covered her hand gently with his other hand and broke into tears. Through the sobs he tried to speak. "I am so...so...sorry!" he gulped. "I didn't want to... I really didn't want to. I wanted nothing to do with this...he made me..."

The guard in the room with them knocked on the door and asked someone on the other side to get a box of tissues.

When one was handed to him, he set it by the prisoner. As he returned to his post behind the prisoner and up against the wall, he shook his head in pity at the broken man.

The prisoner grabbed the tissues after letting go of her hands. She drew them back to rest near her as she clasped them loosely on the table. She waited patiently to let him unburden his soul.

He wiped his face and blew his nose. After the initial outburst of emotions, he calmed slightly and heaved a great sigh. "He made me," he said simply as he kept his face lowered. "He is an evil man. I thought he was my friend. Years ago, I thought he was helping me when I got into some trouble. Instead, he was placing himself in a position to blackmail me."

"Who is this person?" she asked gently as he met her eyes.

"Carlos Lopez," he growled angrily. His hands crushed the sodden tissues as they clenched into fists.

"Carlos Lopez, the well-known financier?" Charlotte asked in surprise. "He's a Keeper?

The prisoner looked at her in surprise. "I don't know what a Keeper is. I had heard him use the term before, but he never explained it," he muttered as he shook his head incredulously. "He's crazy."

Charlotte smiled and nodded. She wouldn't divulge anything more to him about the Keepers or wraiths. She changed the subject. "How long have you known him?"

"We grew up together. Well, at least from high school on. He always seemed older than he was and so wise! That's why I trusted him." He rubbed his eyes as he shook his head. "Same neighborhood. Same school."

Charlotte chewed on her lower lip while she thought, *Must have kept himself younger with a clockworks room to give the illusion of being a teenager.* She focused her attention on the young man on the other side of the table. "While you were growing up, did he ever mention anything about aliens or anything strange?" she asked.

He dropped his hand and looked at her, clearly thinking about her question. "I hadn't thought about that," he muttered, then thought longer. "No. It wasn't until about five or maybe six years ago that he started talking about a secret organization and weird things." He furrowed his brow as he thought further. "He wanted me to join some secret society years back."

Charlotte leaned forward, resting her chin in her hands as she studied him. "Did anything happen around that time? Any event that may have triggered these delusions?"

Dr. Saunders sat back and thought some more as he shook his head slowly. "I don't think so. He was constantly busy building his empires. He was always a bit devious and shady. I suspected the upright businessman image was a front. When I got into trouble, I found he had deep ties to the underworld types."

"Organized crime and such?" she asked quietly.

"Yes," he rubbed his forehead. "I guess he was always bent wrong."

"Yes." She nodded thoughtfully. *That would be fertile ground for growing what we are dealing with now.*

He interrupted her thoughts. "Look, I don't know what's going on. I don't want to know. But you were very important to him. He is afraid of you for whatever reason. He wanted either to be able to control you or for you to be incapacitated enough to stay out of his way."

"But you helped me," she stated simply.

He looked at her sadly. "You didn't deserve being treated like that." He tried to rub his jaw where it was still bruised. The handcuffs clinked metallically as they restricted his movements. "No one deserves that kind of treatment."

"He struck you?"

"Yeah, more than once." He met her eyes; his were deeply sad and resigned. "He will kill me."

Charlotte looked up at the ceiling. Some of the local wraiths had appeared in the room while she was talking with him. She mentally messaged to them that they were to protect this man. They nodded to her that they understood.

The prisoner also looked up at the ceiling trying to see what she was looking at. The guard did, too. They felt silly when she started to talk again as if nothing had happened.

"It'll be best for you stay in confinement for now," she stated simply as she stood. "For your protection."

"Will you be pressing charges?" the constable who was standing guard asked.

"No, I'm after the person who did this to me and to him." She nodded in the prisoner's direction.

"We can't hold him without charging him." The guard pointed out.

Charlotte smiled. "I'll have my lawyer think up a lesser charge for now." She walked to the door.

"Thank you. I don't deserve it," Dr. Saunders said quietly.

"You deserve it," she replied as she turned toward him, hand ready to knock to be let out. "But you need to find a better life and friends."

He nodded in agreement as he looked down at his hands. Then he looked up at her as the door started to open. "Don't you want to know where he is?"

Charlotte smiled as Becker came into the room to report what she had found. The wraith guards in the room, unseen by the other occupants, nodded to her before she turned toward the door to leave the room. "I already know," she said mysteriously and walked out the door. She left behind a mystified copper and prisoner.

CHAPTER FIFTEEN

Charlotte met Grant and Weldon in the hall outside the interrogation room. After the constable escorted them to the exit of the building and left, she told them what Becker had found.

"Our evil Keeper is more evil?" Grant asked when she was done. "Is that what you are telling us?" He looked to Becker. He tried to mentally connect with her to see her impressions directly. She seemed to ignore him.

"Yes, the impression I got from her is that he is more evil than in her last encounter with him," Charlotte added. She was too preoccupied by what she had been told to notice Grant's frustrated expression and question what his problem was.

As they walked outside the building, Weldon pointed them to a car that he had hired. Charlotte was quiet as she was trying to process what Becker told her into better words.

Before Grant got to the car, he turned to Becker. He had had enough and wanted to know what was going on. "Why are you not communicating with me? What is going on?" he asked the black, wispy being following them. In response, she crossed her thin arms across her skeletal chest and glared at him.

Distracted from her thoughts, Charlotte looked from one to the other. "Is she still mad about her clock?" she offered quietly.

"I finished it!" he exclaimed. "It took me a while because of the severe damage and had to have replacement gears cut and parts repaired. The glass and case work also took time. The face had to be redone." He dropped his hands that he had been waving around and stared at the floating wraith. "I can't believe you still are holding a grudge."

Becker responded by turning her back on him. She was upset with him, but it wasn't about her clock. She had gotten frustrated with him for not listening to her when things were intense when Charlotte was in a coma in the hospital. Although she cared for Grant, she didn't think she was jealous of his feelings for Charlotte. She knew they were destined to be together. But she needed him to be back in tune with her. She knew what they were dealing with, and they all needed to be able to communicate with each other without any hindrances.

"Apparently she's not taking your excuses," Weldon observed, his eyebrows lifting while his eyes twinkled in humor. "Or is there another reason?"

Grant huffed in exasperation as he opened the door to the black sedan to let the others in the car. Before he got in, he glared at Becker. "Really?! We have evil running amok and you're still mad at me?" He looked closer at her. "Is it about your clock, or is there something else?"

Becker turned to scowl at him, then winked. She was giving him a hard time now. She had initially contacted Charlotte about the evil Keeper because she was the one most easily accessed. Grant had been too preoccupied. Now, she was trying to figure out why he seemed upset about her not contacting him. Even though her race had coexisted with humans for centuries, they still didn't know much about them. Their ability to completely interact with humans had been limited until the Chosen One emerged. Like the others of her kind, she would experiment with different expressions she saw in humans and watch his responses to develop a system of nonverbal communications. This time, she had imitated the human facial gesture, a wink, to see what reaction she would get.

He stood for a moment in shock. His mouth dropped open. *She winked at me*, he thought as he glanced at Weldon and Charlotte, then back at Becker. "You're stringing me along?" he asked the wraith in surprised realization.

Hovering beside him, she shrugged her thin shoulders. She had stumbled on something she had needed, she had his complete attention. She impressed upon him with the best imagery she could to air her frustrations about not being able to communicate with him when his concentration was intensely on Charlotte. She never revealed to him what risks or pain she had to go through to contact the Chosen One to get things to progress in a timely manner.

His eyes grew wide when he started to understand what she was trying to convey to him. He nodded and mentally apologized. After that, she knew he would think to be more accessible. With that done, she showed him what she had seen at the warehouse.

His mood became somber and serious as he understood what she had seen and was sharing with him. He was about to ask her something when he noted people standing around looking at him strangely.

A crowd had gathered in front of the police station. It had started with the gathering of some of the local Keepers who waited to hear about the results of the interview with one of Charlotte's kidnappers. Other people had been drawn to join them out of curiosity to see what was going on.

As soon as the interview was over, the wraiths in the interrogation room had communicated the details through their network to their Keepers. With this information, the

Keepers were about to disperse when they saw the American Keeper, friend of the Chosen One, being snubbed by his wraith.

As the non-Keeper part of the crowd watched an apparently crazy man argue with thin air, the Keepers watched the interaction between wraith and Keeper, shaking slightly with suppressed laughter as they watched. After a few moments, they signaled to each other to disperse and meet at a predetermined location.

"Get in the car, Grant." Charlotte reached out to grab his pants leg. "People think you are demented."

"He's not?" the driver asked as he watched from the driver's seat.

Weldon lightly slapped him on the arm. "I know you are a Keeper. I saw you at the meeting at the airport."

The dark-haired, dark-eyed man winked at him. "True, mate. I saw this job on the board and volunteered. Thought it would be better to have a driver that is someone in the know." He looked at Charlotte and bowed his head. "I am glad you have recovered." When he smiled, Grant automatically looked for a gold tooth. Not seeing one, he relaxed into the back seat.

"I got a message that the Keepers were gathering," the driver told them as he faced forward to start the car. "I will take you there," he said over his shoulder as he merged the sedan into traffic.

"Thank you." Charlotte answered automatically. She had slipped back into her thoughts and looked distracted and worried.

They met with the other Keepers from the area in a back room of a pub. Charlotte was so distracted by her internal turmoil that she didn't notice the men already seated at several of the blocky, wooden tables scattered around the large, utilitarian room. She had no idea that they watched her with star-struck interest and attentive deference. But Grant did. As they were seated at a table near the wall opposite the doorway, he grumbled to Weldon. "They act like she's a rock star."

Weldon sat next to his granddaughter against the wall and watched as other men came into the room. They seated themselves in a hushed manner, as if they were entering into a church. "They do seem to be in awe," he observed in a whisper to Grant who had sat across the table from him with his back to the other Keepers.

Weldon looked up to see a tall gentleman enter and scan the room as if he were taking roll of who was present. His slender frame with long arms and legs sported a finely tailored suit. As his sweeping gaze faced their table, Weldon recognized the newcomer's lean, clean-shaven face that sprouted a long, aristocratic nose. He had seen Charlotte and started to walk toward them. Weldon gestured for Grant to turn around to see him approach.

"Hello, Piers," Grant greeted him once he saw who approached them. He smiled and stood up to shake hands with the English lord.

"Hello, Grant." The richly cultured, British accent added class to the greeting. "This must be the lady we've heard so much about," he said as he bowed to Charlotte.

Weldon saw that Charlotte was still distracted and nudged her. Focusing on the distinguished gentleman, she smiled. "Glad to meet you face to face, Lord Holmes," she said as she extended her hand to shake his.

"My pleasure." He smiled, then bowed to Weldon. "Sir Weldon Gregory, I have been wondering where you were hiding. I must say I was pleasantly shocked to find out that you are one of us!"

Weldon stood to bow and shake his hand. "The subject never had come up, I suppose. I wish it had. Thought I was running a bit batty!"

Piers smiled and laughed as he clapped him on the shoulder. "You are looking in fine shape. I'm glad you found out who you truly were in time for the wraiths to help stop the aging process!"

Grant was looking from one to the other in confusion. "You two know each other?"

"Oh," Piers said companionably. "We've known each other from way back."

Weldon shook his head in memory. "The war, Grant, the war."

Grant was going to ask which one, but caught the twinkle in Piers' eye. He knew the lord had seen every war since the War of the Roses and decided not to broach that memory lane.

"But we grew apart," Weldon muttered as he looked at Piers, his face unreadable.

Piers laughed. "Oh, it is no matter now!" He faced Grant to explain. "He stole my manservant from me years ago!" He shook his head as he smiled. "Winston has since been in touch with me. He reported that he is in fine fettle. Seems to have a new lease on life and happy to be in your household."

"You did a good job keeping the secret from him," Weldon said as he gestured for Piers to sit down at the table.

Piers nodded. "It was hard. He is such an exacting fellow." He waved a hand, indicating that he would remain standing. The men continued to stand with him.

"He knows about them now."

Piers stopped to look at Grant, who had revealed this information. "Can he see them?"

Weldon shook his head. "No, he simply figured something must be happening because of the change he's seen in me."

Piers nodded thoughtfully. "Yes. Yes. That's right! I had forgotten that I had heard you were at death's door." He studied Weldon even closer. "The clockwork rooms can do that much?" He looked away, his expression somber, his eyes unfocused as if to gaze at something far off. "I never realized they were that powerful."

"Powerful enough to kill you if they are destroyed," Grant muttered darkly.

Piers' face tensed grimly as he nodded at Grant. "It is a dangerous thing. We must be extra careful to secure our rooms." He looked back at Weldon. "Why didn't your wraiths offer to help you build a room years ago?" he asked sharply as his eyebrows raised high in indignation.

Weldon hung his head. "They did try to tell me." He shook his head sadly. "But I couldn't comprehend...no, I didn't believe...what they were indicating it would do." He looked up at Piers. "It's too fantastical!"

Piers clapped a hand on his shoulder. "That is true, but it is real."

"Now I know." Weldon looked thoughtful. "I also remember that they wanted me to talk to Grant. I was too scared to ask for fear I would seem crazy."

"Seems wraiths are very loyal to their Keepers," Grant said quietly. "They respected your wishes, so they didn't contact me directly."

"They are a deeply mysterious race of beings," Piers muttered thoughtfully.

Charlotte was still seated but was listening to their conversation. "More than you know," she whispered. Her feminine voice, even quietly spoken, could be heard above the masculine murmurings that had started up in the room after Lord Holmes had arrived. When they heard her, they stopped talking to watch her in attentive silence.

Grant moved to sit by her. He recognized the look on her face. "More has been revealed to you?" he whispered.

She tried to smile, then rubbed her eyes with one hand. "It is blurry, like a half-remembered dream. But there is something more. Something I need to do or find." She fell silent again as she returned to her thoughts.

Piers cleared his throat and called the meeting to order. He decided not to call on her to speak unless she felt that she needed to tell them something.

Standing near her table, Piers started to talk. "As you all have been told, the evil Keeper we have been searching for since the 'Day of the Wraith' has been found. Unfortunately, he is in possession of a freestanding tower clock movement in which he has trapped a Sentinel. It has been confirmed that this Sentinel is the one that had inhabited the Great Clock, known as Big Ben, before it was shut down for renovations."

Many of them were surprised by the news of the missing Sentinel, as this information had not been revealed to all the Keepers until this meeting. Their reaction was quick but hushed as they anticipated what was going to come up next.

All ears were in tune to their local leader, but their eyes were still watching Charlotte.

"We need to coordinate efforts between wraiths and Keepers to storm the building, free the Sentinel, and capture the evil Keeper and all his wraiths."

"We have no working vaults," one man spoke up from the group.

"Hopefully, once the Sentinel is freed, he can trap them in the tower clock mechanism he now inhabits," Piers said confidently.

"Can another Sentinel come in and help?" another voice asked.

Piers glanced at Charlotte. "It is unknown at this time. There are not many of us who can communicate with them."

Grant whispered to Charlotte. "Do you think the others can help?" He wasn't sure if she was hearing the conversation.

She slowly shook her head. "They are territorial. The ones I have contacted indicated they have a certain area they are to guard. They are made for heavy combat, not for long distance flight. They have to stay close to their clockworks." Although she spoke quietly to answer Grant, her voice carried in the silent room and was heard by the others.

Grant shook his head at Piers as the lord watched them to confirm what he had heard. The question was answered, but it was bleak. For the plan to work, they had to free the Sentinel and hope he would be able to trap the others.

"What if the Sentinel has been turned to evil?" another voice asked.

"The information we have is that so far it has not, but time is of the essence," Piers answered.

Charlotte stood up. The sound of her chair scooting back against the hardwood floor alerted Piers. He stayed silent and moved to the side, giving her the floor.

"The Sentinel has been under intense pressure by an entity of pure evil. Because of this, he has separated into individual beings. However, those wraiths will not survive for long. They are not complete because they have been bonded for centuries." She walked to the middle of the room. "If he can rebond, he may be too weak to help. This may have to be an operation to save him and deal with the others later."

"Can you tell if he can survive?" Piers asked her.

"It is unknown at this time," she said sadly. "The reports I'm getting are very dire."

"How should we proceed?" the lord asked her quietly.

She looked over at him. "Brute force?" She threw out the question with a shrug. "I don't know." She looked around the room. "Do you all know of the great evil?"

Most of the Keepers nodded. Some looked skeptical. One voiced his disbelief. "What is that supposed to mean?"

"It is pure evil. It is what led to the destruction of their society and what made them flee their home environment and adopt ours."

She looked around the room and saw that none of them 'got it.' Even if they believed, they didn't understand the scope of the danger. She ran her fingers through her hair, further tousling the mop of dark blond curls. *I can't worry about their lack of belief or whatever,* she thought to herself in frustration. *There is something I need to do, but what is it?* The thought niggled at her; it pulled at her. But she was directionless. She wouldn't find answers where she was with a room full of Keepers but no answers. She had to leave them to figure out what she needed to do. She was about to leave when a thought hit her. "Does anyone know where an Oracle is?"

Every man in the room looked at her, mystified. *Oh great,* she thought, *they think I'm nuts.* She smiled and said more confidently than she felt, "I'll find one." She quickly walked out of the room. As she stepped through the doorway into the pub itself, she heard men's voices start to mutter and soon rise in volume as they discussed all that they had heard.

Grant had stood while she was talking to the group. When she walked out of the room, he followed. Glancing back, Weldon waved him on. He would stay and monitor what the Keepers were planning.

After following her through the crowded pub, he caught up with her as she stood at the curb, looking around. Becker was hovering near her. As he slipped up to stand next to her, she looked over at him. "May I go with you?" he asked quietly, still not sure if she wanted him around or not. He was relieved when she smiled and nodded.

She slipped her arm through his. Reaching up, she whispered to him, "Becker knows where I need to go. I need to go to a street clock built in 1888 on Harlesden High Street in Brent. I believe it is one of the Jubilee clocks commemorating Queen Victoria's Golden Jubilee."

Although he had been hoping for tender words of heartfelt emotion, Grant was happy with the fact that he could be with her and that she asked for his help. Without hesitation, he hailed a taxi. Once they got in the cab, he gave the instructions to the driver and sat back with Charlotte beside him. Becker was outside the cab as she paced alongside it. As they rode in silence, he wondered what they were going to find when they reached the street clock.

CHAPTER SIXTEEN

Soon they stood in front of the red and gold ornate pedestal street clock. Each of the Roman numeral faces displayed the time to four different directions. As he studied it in detail, Grant admired the craftsmanship and longed to study the movement. He sighed as he realized he hadn't really noticed street clocks before. "I really need to join the NAWCC chapter 134 for tower clocks and street clocks," he muttered to himself.

When he stood near the pedestal of the freestanding clock, he could sense a presence, but it was different from what he had ever experienced before. It was not the presence of a Time Wraith, and it was not the powerful, foreboding presence of a Sentinel. It was mysterious and compelling. The overall effect raised the hairs on the back of his neck and arms.

He looked down to see that Charlotte was gazing at one of the ornate faces. After a while, she touched the clock's post. A wraith-like being came up from out of the ground. Instead of the black wispy substance of a typical wraith, it was a form made of silvery sand-like essence. He also saw that she glittered as she hovered in front of Charlotte. She was also slightly larger than Becker, who floated nearby.

He saw that Charlotte was in deep communication with what he assumed was the Oracle. Slowly, he turned to watch the surrounding people, shops, and streets. That was when he noticed that Becker had stationed wraiths around them as guards.

* * * * * * *

Charlotte stood patiently as the alien before her probed her. She felt her presence drifting through her thoughts and mind, searching her intentions and her heart. Then the mysterious wraith spoke.

"You are truly the Chosen One," the Oracle's voice was feminine but deep, mellow, and warm, like heated honey. "Your task is at hand," she spoke slowly, allowing each word to sink in. She recognized that Charlotte had been shocked to actually hear a voice in her mind instead of images. "But the end of the task is not swift. The resolution is not certain." She stopped for a bit and looked at Becker, then back at Charlotte. "You need to find the orb containing the hope for all." As she started to stream back into the street clock, her voice trailed off into a hollow echo, "It must be found or all is lost. Look to the pillar that weeps and where wishes are placed."

When the Oracle had fully integrated back into the street clock, Charlotte looked up to Becker. The Time Wraith shook her head and shrugged her shoulders when asked about the orb.

Charlotte looked around the area and noted Grant standing guard. She was glad he was with her. Seeing him when she awoke from what seemed to be an endless, but unremembered, nightmare had warmed her heart. He was her sentinel, and she knew that she belonged at his side and nowhere else. She looked away to glance at the street clock again. She suddenly had a sharp and deep foreboding that his feelings for her would be tested before the resolution of the current crisis.

Taking a deep breath, she shook off the dark feeling and moved closer to him. He looked down at her and smiled. "Did you find out what you need?"

She half-smiled and shrugged slightly. "In a cryptic way." She looked around as she thought about what she was told. "Do you know anything about an orb?"

"Orb?" Grant asked; his brow furrowed, drawing his eyebrows together. "What kind of orb? That is an extremely nondescript and vague reference."

Moving away from the street clock as she thought about her encounter with the mysterious wraith, she started to walk down the street, looking at the shops nearby. Grant matched her pace as they talked. When she took his arm and moved closer to him, she noticed his reaction as his smile brightened and lit up his face.

"It has something in it that we need for this task," she explained, her voice low.

"Did she say what?" Grant asked as he glanced up and saw that the wraiths were moving with them, keeping an eye out for trouble, whether human or otherwise.

"She said it 'had the hope for all,'" she said as she formed air quotes with her fingers.

"Any other clues?" Grant asked quickly as he glanced down at her. He looked up to see that they were approaching an intersection. He slowed his pace and felt Charlotte slowing down with him.

"She did say something about 'looking to the pillar that weeps and where wishes are left' or something like that," she said as they stopped at the corner.

Still deep in their conversation, they stood on the corner as traffic passed by them. Grant shook his head slowly as he thought. "I'm not sure where to start."

"Neither do I," Charlotte said sadly. She looked up and down the streets from the intersection and motioned for them to walk around the corner. They were walking about aimlessly as they pondered their next move.

After they walked for a while in silence, Grant asked, "Do we need to find this before we release the Sentinel? It sounds as if we need to help him as quickly as possible."

She looked off into the distance as she contemplated his question. "I do feel we need to save the Sentinel and then deal with the evil one."

Just then Grant's cell rang. Continuing to walk, he took it out of his pocket and saw that it was Weldon. "What's the news?" Grant answered.

"We're moving in on the warehouse in a few hours," Weldon answered, then paused. Grant could hear voices and commotion in the background. "Will you be going in?"

Grant had put him on speaker phone. Charlotte nodded. "Yes," he answered.

"Need directions?"

Grant looked up at Becker. She hovered near him, arms crossed as she glared at him. She looked at him as if she were daring him to ignore her again.

"Oh, no! We have Becker with us," he said as he smiled up at her. He was rewarded with a satisfied nod and smile. He nodded back, glad that his wraith seemed appeased.

"Good. See you there."

After Grant disconnected and slipped his cell into his pocket, he hailed a passing taxi. Once they got settled in their seats, Grant had the cabbie start driving as he gave directions, following Becker as she guided them through the city.

As a result of the piecemeal directions, the driver was steaming mad when they reached their destination, an abandoned-looking, graffiti-covered warehouse in Wandsworth borough. "Why couldn't you have just given me the address? Or at least told me what you were looking for?!"

They didn't say anything as they got out of the cab. Grant paid the fare and added a huge tip to it. He smiled to himself as he saw the cabbie's eyes widen at the thick roll of bills he was handed. Glancing around and seeing that there was no one around but Charlotte, he couldn't resist some harmless fun. He slowly leaned down to whisper into the man's ear. "I'm a psychic and had to follow directions as they came to me."

"Oh," the driver whispered as he sat in shock with a palm full of money. Grant smiled mysteriously as he stood up and walked to where Charlotte was standing. As they both turned to walk away from the taxi, Grant looked back to see the driver snap out of his trance, quickly stash away the cash as if it was about to be taken from him, and burn rubber to leave the area.

Grant muffled a laugh as he shook his head. He glanced at Charlotte when she stopped walking, then did a double take. She was standing rigid, totally focused on the large brick building. Her face was blanched and tight with pain. Tears formed in her eyes.

He moved to put an arm around her. She leaned into him but stayed rigid.

"He's dying," she muttered with despair. "We can't wait for the others. It'll be too late."

Grant slipped his arm from around her to move toward the building. He waved Becker over to ask her telepathically what she had seen in the warehouse. He had her repeat it until he had a feel for the dimensions and layout of the area.

When they were done, he had her move her team to seal off the perimeter.

"Okay," he told Charlotte, who had been watching him. "We're going to go to the back of the warehouse. The wraiths will follow us in."

She gulped, then nodded. She was afraid that she might have to confront her captor again. But the weak cries of the wraiths that made up the once powerful Sentinel beckoned her more strongly than her fears kept her away. "Okay." She nodded at him as she steeled herself. "Let's go."

CHAPTER SEVENTEEN

The evil-entity-possessed Carlos had been sitting with the other Keepers in the back room of the pub. It had a need to see what it was up against in this new world of strangers. It had found out about the meeting from the wraiths it had sent to spy on the Keepers. Once it had hustled over to the pub, it had no problems slipping into the room as it was filling up. It simply acted as if it belonged there, and if anyone looked at Carlos' body too long, it waved and greeted them as if it knew him.

From its vantage point in the crowd, it watched Charlotte throughout the meeting, first as she sat brooding and then when she stood up and spoke to the group. The entity knew that Carlos was both very attracted and repelled by her and couldn't understand those human emotions. It saw that she had men close to her. As it picked through its prisoner's memories, it found out who they were. Grant, the clock shop owner who had foiled Carlos' original plan for world domination and also her grandfather, who no one had known was a Keeper and also was another reason Carlos' plans had failed.

The entity understood hate and anger. With them, it fueled itself from Carlos' seething fury at these individuals. As it allowed the human's dark emotions to make it stronger, it was careful to shield the resulting intensification of its evil power from the Keepers who surrounded him. It didn't want to spring its surprise too soon by letting them sense who it was.

When Charlotte had asked about the Oracle, it was curious but not concerned. It wasn't aware of anything in the Society that would serve as an oracle, so it dismissed the idea and caused Carlos' body to whisper to those around him that she was crazy. It was happy to see that it turned some of the disbelievers against her. It smiled to itself as it had Carlos sit back with his arms crossed over his chest and watch the action.

After a few moments, it had a niggling thought that Carlos hadn't been aware of the Sentinels, either, until it was too late. Its moment of glee passed, and it started to seethe again. When it noticed the Keepers around it acting restless and looking around, the entity dialed back its anger and tightened its grip on its evil nature to tightly bottle it up so they could no longer sense it.

After Charlotte had left, it stayed to hear the plans of the Keepers and plot its response. When it heard the time table of when they would be storming the warehouse, it laughed to itself. It would be ready for them. It contacted its wraiths and laid out the plan to not only defend the building but also to crush all the Keepers and their wraiths in an ambush.

The evil presence laughed with sharp-edged hysterics in Carlos' mind as it insinuated itself with a small group as the Keepers left the pub to disperse throughout the city. The plan was to have several groups of Keepers and wraiths coordinate an attack on the warehouse from multiple fronts. When there were no further details to the plan, the entity caused Carlos to slip away without being noticed. Before it directed its host to go back to the warehouse to put its plan into action, it decided it had plenty of time to do some mischief while it was out and about in its prisoner's body.

Little did the entity know that Grant and Charlotte were ahead of schedule.

CHAPTER EIGHTEEN

Grant and Charlotte gingerly stepped through waist-high weeds and trash to sneak around the large, dilapidated brick building. All the rusted metal doors were firmly locked or rusted shut. Although there were many broken windows, they were high above them on the crumbling, red brick walls. Once they rounded the corner to the back facing the river front, they saw their entry point. A large window of filthy glass that was low enough to the ground for them to reach with minimal effort. Its glass was intact but was partially open.

Grant boosted Charlotte up to the window to wrench it open further. They both stopped and froze when the rusted metal of the window mechanism shrieked in protest as it stubbornly yielded to her. When they didn't hear anyone coming to investigate the noise, Grant helped her through the opening, then followed by pulling himself up from the bottom frame of the window. Soon they both were standing in the dimly lit storage area of the warehouse. As they peered around the large room, trying to see detail in the heavily shadowed areas, all they could make out was one structure in the man-made cavern.

They hesitated before moving as they looked at each other in surprise, barely able to see each other's face in the gloom. They had expected some resistance from wraith guards. Not seeing any hints of danger, they abandoned caution and ran to the structure where they found the tower clock movement entrapped in a metal cage.

They were shocked and surprised by the extreme condition in which they found the Sentinel. His separate selves could barely be seen as they lay scattered around the movement within the metal cage.

"They look like dead flies around a bug zapper," Charlotte cried out as tears welled up in her eyes. She held her hands to her open mouth as she tried to hold in the sobs of horror for the formerly magnificent being.

Grant had to agree with her assessment. He was angry and sad, both reactions in equal intensities. He had seen a Sentinel in full form and vigor. This wretched mess was a battered, tormented shadow of his intended power and form.

He studied the cage closely to see if there was a door that could be opened. He quickly realized that the cage was made up of the metallic silver grey cubes that he had seen in action before. He made note that the open top of the cage came up to him at chest level. The four walls surrounding the clockworks were a foot thick on all sides. He quickly estimated that it would take hundreds, if not thousands, of the one-inch cubes to make a cage this large.

Where does he get these things? he couldn't help wondering to himself. "So that's what it would take to trap a Sentinel," he muttered darkly as he started to break down the cage. He grabbed handfuls of the metallic cubes and threw them so violently that many of them hit the nearby brick walls and bounced off in all directions. Charlotte quickly joined in. In no time, they had cleared the cage away.

After the barrier was gone, Grant noticed that the tower clock movement had stopped. Searching around, he soon found the crank hanging on the clockworks' green metal support frame. He quickly wound it to bring the weight up so as to power the time chain as gravity pulled it steadily down. Setting the crank down, he pushed the pendulum to restart it. The slow tick-tock filled the giant room as the static time train became active.

"They're too weak to merge together and enter the movement!" Charlotte cried as she focused on the wraiths around their feet and seeing how they were getting weaker by the second. "And they cannot enter such a powerful movement by themselves!"

Grant scanned around the large warehouse space. There wasn't another mechanical clock in sight. "What do we use for power? They need a smaller clockwork mechanism to strengthen." He started to pace around the room as he tried to figure out what to do. He thought about calling on the local Keepers to bring small clocks or pocket watches with them, but he trashed that idea, knowing they were running out of time. Not only were the wraiths in their last few moments of life, he figured Carlos would be arriving any moment and would interfere with any such plan.

Charlotte looked around as well. She ran to the front of the building and searched through the offices hoping to find a forgotten timepiece from bygone days. She rejoined Grant empty-handed as she shook her bowed head in defeat.

They had nothing except the tower clock movement, and it was too powerful for the separated wraiths in their state. They were there to help but had no way to help them. They felt absolutely powerless in the situation.

In despair, all they could do was look at each other, then watch the dying wraiths. Their hearts were torn and crying for these beings. They both felt the specter of panic grip their minds in its freezing clutches, preventing them from thought or action.

Instinctively, Charlotte moved toward Grant, needing his strength. He wrapped his arms around her as he pulled her close to him, her head resting on his chest. Her nearness was a balm and strength to him, enabling him to force his mind out of the morass of fear to work furiously on the problem.

Charlotte watched the writhing wraiths from the shelter of Grant's arms. As she tried to think of a way to help them, she became more aware of Grant's heartbeat drumming in her ear. "Heartbeat," she muttered to herself. She pulled away from Grant to look into his anxious face. "Heartbeat," she said louder. They met each other's eyes and saw in each other a mutual understanding. A ray of hope stabbed through the darkness of the situation.

"They were drawn here…" Charlotte started.

"By the beat of the human heart," Grant finished.

"It could hurt us…" she was starting to say as she lifted a finger at him.

Grant interrupted her, "But we don't know that." His face was set on the course of action they knew had to be done.

Charlotte nodded as her attitude morphed from caution to determination. "It wouldn't matter," she said as she stepped toward Grant. "We're going to do it anyway."

Grant moved closer to her again. Without a word, they faced each other and held hands tightly. They each took a deep breath while they closed their eyes, then telepathically reached out to connect to as many of the wraiths as they could.

At first, they felt the reluctance of the wraiths. They were sworn not to harm humans. But Grant and Charlotte continued to insist that it must be done. Their mental voices echoed each other's as they kept repeating that the wraiths needed to be strong enough to become whole. To rejoin. To become the Sentinel again.

Finally, a compromise was reached. The dying wraiths agreed that only a few of them at a time would merge with the human couple. This would only last as long as they needed to be strong enough to link together. From there, they felt they would be able to enter the tower clock mechanism to regain their full strength as a Sentinel.

Becker had watched Grant and Charlotte from the sidelines. As soon as her team surrounded the warehouse, she had come inside to see what was happening. She knew that what they were planning to do was extremely risky. Risky enough that the humans and all the wraiths involved could die in the attempt. She sent up a quick prayer to the Power Above All, then informed her team of what was going on. She emphasized to them the importance that none of the enemy break through their perimeter. She knew that those involved would be vulnerable during the process, and she wanted to be as ready as possible if the evil Keeper or his wraiths came back.

The first few dying wraiths started off barely touching the couple. When they saw the humans were ready, willing, and strong enough, they fully merged with both of them. As soon as the process started, Grant and Charlotte were instantly linked mentally through them. Memories of their pasts were experienced by the other. Grant was able to see her childhood, the first encounter with a wraith, and her life events up to when they met. She was able to see the hundreds of years of his life and his personal witness to the events in history.

They didn't know how much time had passed when the memory link started to fade. When they became aware of their surroundings again, they saw all the weak wraiths were gone. As they turned toward the tower clock movement, they could sense a powerful presence building within the depths of the clockworks. They turned to smile at each other and sigh in joint relief that the merging seemed to have worked. Then they shared secret, intimate smiles as they both recognized that the merging had formed a deep link between the two of them.

Becker swooped in to hover near them. She studied them intensely as she looked them over. After a while, she smiled her smoky smile and nodded to them. She looked relieved that they were all right.

"He's going to have a nasty shock," Charlotte said, smiling, as she turned to look at the large clockwork mechanism again. She continued to hold one of Grant's hands as she moved. Grant was reluctant to let her go but had to so that he could start preparing for the evil Keeper's arrival.

"We need to make it look as if nothing has been disturbed," he explained as he scooped up an arm full of the dull silver cubes.

"How?" Charlotte asked. She was mystified but started to do as he was doing. She figured an explanation would be next.

"Rebuild the cage so it looks complete from the front, but leave the back open."

"So the Sentinel can emerge." Charlotte nodded, showing she liked the idea. "What do we do with the extra cubes?"

Grant looked around the large room and at the pile of cubes still on the floor from the destroyed cage. "Let's start with rebuilding the cage. I may have an idea what to do with them, if we have enough left over to do the job."

They worked as quickly as they could. Soon the metal cage was rebuilt to look as if it hadn't been touched. No one seeing it from the front could see any changes unless he walked around the back.

Grant contemplated the pile of cubes left over. He scanned the floor of the large room from the open double doors coming from the front offices to the metal cage. "I think we can use these, as long as we space them apart to enclose a large area on the floor."

Charlotte cocked her head as she looked at the cubes, at the floor, and then at him. "What do you hope to accomplish?"

"Trapping the evil wraiths," he said quietly. He contacted Becker to see if she and her team would be willing to test it. Becker looked dubious but nodded her head to accept his plan.

Grant grabbed some more cubes and directed Charlotte to do the same. They made a circle as large as they could with the cubes spaced a couple of feet from each other. After they formed it, they opened up a large gap. Becker and her team moved to within the circle. Repositioning the cubes to enclose the circle again, Grant signaled Becker to try to get out. Without effort, all of them were able to escape as soon as the signal was given.

Grant rubbed his chin as he thought. "There must be a minimal distance for them to work together." He motioned Charlotte to help him move the cubes closer together and try again. When that didn't work, they tried again, and again. Only when the cubes were less than a foot from each other was the circle complete enough that none of the wraiths could pass through it. They opened up a gap and let them out.

"How are we going to complete the circle without their seeing it?" Charlotte wondered aloud as she studied the ring of metallic cubes.

Grant contemplated the setup as he paced around the room. His eyes had fully adjusted to the meager light and were able to see the single chair and small table near the middle of the room. He gauged the distance from them to the clockworks. "He must be sitting here to watch the Sentinel." He pointed to the chair then paced the area around the furniture. He kicked some of the cubes over to form a ring between the chair and the tower clockworks. "If we leave part of it set up, all we have to do is complete it once the wraiths are in it."

Charlotte helped him move the cubes to their new location. Once it was formed, they removed a third of them to open the ring. All they could do was hope the remaining arc wouldn't be noticed by the evil Keeper. Grant found an old burlap bag and put the remaining cubes into it.

"Becker, let the other wraiths know of the plan so they can concentrate the enemy wraiths within the ring," Grant instructed the hovering wraith. He turned to Charlotte. "When the other Keepers get here, we will get them to help close up the circle."

"Our wraiths are going to be trapped as well," Charlotte pointed out, biting her lower lip as she walked around the room, studying the set up.

Grant looked to the tower clock mechanism. "From what you have told me about Sentinels in battle, he will be able to tell which is which."

Charlotte nodded as she remembered the battle in the town square. That Sentinel knew which ones to grab and place in his cage of lightning and shadow and which ones to leave alone.

Suddenly, they heard the door at the front of the warehouse open and shut. They froze as they looked at each other in indecision, hearing footsteps coming down the hall toward them. They weren't sure whether it was friend or foe. Without a sound, they ran to stand behind the open double doors leading into the large room. Because of the small space, they split up to hide until they could see who was approaching.

Becker and her team dispersed to hide in the walls. She had already contacted the other wraiths in the area with the details of the plan. She relayed a message back to Grant that they were already converging on the warehouse with their Keepers. Grant nodded as he got her message.

Once they were behind the doors, Charlotte sensed the evil before the person even got into the room. She was relieved that they had decided to hide. This person was not a friend.

CHAPTER NINETEEN

Carlos sauntered through the door. Dark green miasma encircled him in an evil aura. Even though she didn't see him immediately, Charlotte quickly grew sickened with his presence as he passed close by. She leaned against the wall with her head back and her feet braced against the door. She was thankful the doors had been latched open with sturdy catches wedged into the concrete floor. After a few minutes, she was able to take slow, deep breaths to help steady herself without giving her position away. She was glad Grant couldn't see the state she was in and wondered if this presence of pure evil affected him as badly. Even though Becker had told her that Carlos was possessed by this great evil and she had had visions of the great evil destroying the original society of the wraiths, she had not been prepared enough for what she sensed as he merely passed by.

Both large metal doors had windows that afforded them a line of sight into the room. Grant figured they had been a safety feature of a working warehouse so that the workers could see if anyone was standing near the doors before they moved a load in or out of the storage area. Even though the evil Keeper could have seen them if he had looked back, he never bothered since he didn't expect anyone to be there except the tortured Sentinel.

Carlos had stopped in the middle of the room by the chair and table. He seemed to be fully focused on the tower clock movement and hadn't noticed anything else. His wraiths came to hover around him. They hadn't noticed anything amiss, so great was their fear of the evil entity.

"Now, remember," the evil entity ordered them, its inhuman voice, like grating metal, torturing the air with its utterance. "This is supposed to be a surprise attack! Now act surprised when they come in." It laughed harshly and long. "Go into the walls and jump out when those Keepers and their wraiths come rushing in. I want to make sure they enjoy my party." It laughed again as it caused Carlos' body to sit down in the chair. "I want to work on our big friend here. Apparently, he got himself back together."

Both Grant and Charlotte breathed a sigh of relief when Carlos paid no attention to the arc of cubes between his seat and the giant clockworks. Their relief quickly turned into a horrified fascination as they watched a sickly, dark green cloud flow out of Carlos and toward the ticking mechanism.

When they recovered from their shock, they both felt that they needed to step in and help the newly bonded Sentinel. As they hesitated to reveal themselves while they tried to form some sort of plan, they noticed that the sinister cloud had stopped near the cage. They held their breath as it hovered, its shape expanding and contracting like a breathing being.

It was hard to determine why the entity had stopped. Did it sense them? Did it wonder why the Sentinel was back in the movement? Could it not decide what to do? None of that mattered as within a few moments the Keepers and their wraiths rushed in through the front of the building and rappelled through all the windows in the storage area.

Quick as a knee-jerk reflex, the evil cloud shot out a tentacle that grabbed Carlos. In response, like a puppet controlled by its puppeteer, he turned in his chair to greet them. "Welcome! Meet my surprise party." His face stretched into a maniacal grin as the grating-metal voice spoke.

As the Keepers stopped in surprise, the bad wraiths poured out of the walls to attack the wraiths that had just come in with their Keepers. The shrieking masses of smoky, sand-like clouds writhed and twisted in midair while the battle raged fiercely. Suddenly, another wave of wraiths came out of the other walls to join the battle. Grant recognized Becker and her team before they joined in the melee. They circled the others and focused on pushing all the battling wraiths into the area where the circle of silvery cubes would be completed.

The groups of Keepers split up. Some rushed at Carlos while the others helped Charlotte and Grant place the silvery cubes to quickly complete the circle. With that the wraiths were trapped.

Carlos had run away from the Keepers when they had rushed at him and headed toward the tower clock mechanism. Even though he was still tethered by a tentacle, he stopped suddenly as he neared the hovering, ugly, green cloud. Before the Keepers could get to him, he suddenly turned around and sprinted toward the open double doors like a linebacker as he shoved everyone out of his way. He was running not only from them but also from the evil presence that seemed to be getting larger as the fighting raged nearby.

The evil entity was enjoying the nearby conflict and had no worries about the humans who were filling the area. It was unhappy that Carlos was trying to run away and did not want to lose its prize catch. It thickened its tentacle and was in the process of shooting out more of them after the running figure, when its hold and concentration were abruptly broken.

A huge, black, smoky arm had shot out of the tower clockworks to clutch the green cloud in a mighty fist. The rest of the Sentinel, whole and powerful, followed swiftly after. He wrestled with the evil presence, but it writhed and screamed as it wriggled out of his grasp. After it escaped and dodged the Sentinel's grasping hands, the evil presence shot up through the ceiling and was gone.

Without skipping a beat, the Sentinel wasted no time to get to his next task. He quickly formed his cage of lightning and shadow. After he swatted the shadowy cloud of battling wraiths apart, he started to grab each one with lightening-fast jabs. Once he had a hold of each one, he would study them quickly and either let them go or thrust them into his cage. Soon the ring of silver cubes was empty.

Once his task was completed, he studied the ceiling where the evil entity had departed. Looking around the room, he didn't register the Keepers watching him until his eyes landed on Charlotte standing by Grant. He nodded once at her, then flowed inside the movement as he dragged the cage in with him.

After the Sentinel was back in the tower clockworks, the Keepers started to consult the wraiths and each other as they compared notes. After a while, several of them removed the remains of the metal cage and picked up the cubes lying on the floor. They were able to find more bags and hauled the rest away.

Charlotte walked over to look out the door through which Carlos had fled. Chewing her lower lip, she studied the ceiling where the sickly green cloud had gone. She could feel nothing more of its presence.

Grant was talking with some of the other Keepers about what had happened when he saw her alone. He could tell she was thinking about something that worried her. He went to be with her.

"Carlos Lopez," he said, trying to get her attention. She looked at him blankly, her mind still elsewhere. "The evil Keeper?" he specified as he watched her face closely for any sign of response.

She focused on him and smiled. "Oh, yes." Her face looked pensive again. "Yes, that is the name Dr. Saunders had told us. Now we know what he looks like."

"What's wrong?" he asked as concern colored his voice. She was acting distant.

She looked up at him, then the other Keepers. After a few minutes, she turned back to him. "We call him the evil Keeper, but there is a more evil presence than he is."

"That creepy miasma that oozed out of him?" Grant asked. "Becker had warned us that he was possessed by something."

She nodded. "I am certain that presence was not with him before."

"How can you be sure?" Grant asked quietly. "You were drugged."

"I am not absolutely sure. But if that evil entity had been present, he would've killed me, not just drugged me."

Grant looked at her for a while. "Why do you think that?"

"That thing is the great evil that destroyed their society," she whispered hoarsely. "But it is more powerful, more intense than before."

Before Grant could react Weldon came over to join them. "Carlos Lopez. I couldn't believe it was him until I saw him." he was muttering. "I used to do business with him until I found out he was shady."

"Did any of the others know of him?" Grant asked.

Weldon nodded. "He showed up in this area a few years ago. Showed he knew enough of the wraiths that they felt he had been elsewhere."

"Elsewhere?" Grant asked.

"Well, unknown, undiscovered," Weldon tried to explain. "They're not sure if he's been associated with Keepers in other areas around the world. He may have been hiding amongst them, doing who knows what, over unknown spans of time.

"Not like you? Were you considered 'elsewhere?'" Grant teased him gently.

Weldon shook his head. "No, my situation still mystifies other Keepers." His face grew serious as he looked from Grant to Charlotte and back again. "Was that ugly green cloud what I think it was?"

"If you mean the great evil I mentioned before, you are correct," Charlotte said quietly to her grandfather.

Weldon nodded, then gestured to the remaining Keepers who had their heads together, talking about something serious. "Many of them now believe you, but some are still in denial about what they saw."

Grant shrugged. "That is the way with some people. You show them something they cannot deny, but they still do because it doesn't fit into their reality."

Weldon watched the other Keepers for a while and then looked up at the ceiling where the miasma had escaped. "I wonder where it came from. It is certainly not of this world."

Charlotte shook her head as she muttered, "It came from the wraith's home environment. I don't know how it came to earth."

Grant reacted by shrugging his shoulders as he looked around. "I have no idea." That creepy black-green cloud was the stuff of nightmares that he would rather not think further about. His attention focused on the tower clockworks that was completely cleared of the metallic cubes. "What is going to happen to the movement?"

"One of the local Keepers knows of a place where it can be kept safe and guarded," Weldon said.

"Everyone knows once the clock in Big Ben is refurbished and returned to its tower, he'll go back to it," Grant commented as he watched the tower clock tick steadily. "This one is a much smaller mechanism than his usual home."

Weldon looked over at Charlotte. "Are we done here?" he asked quietly.

She met her grandfather's eyes. "We are done here," she said firmly.

Weldon looked relieved and smiled. "So we can go home?" he asked hopefully.

Even though the evil Keeper was at large and the great evil had come to earth, Grant was starting to smile with the thought of going home for a breather, until he heard her answer. "No. We need to go to Turkey."

"Turkey?!" Weldon asked sharply in surprise. "Why Turkey?"

She held up her smart phone to show them. "We need to go to Hagia Sophia in Istanbul."

Grant took her phone and looked at the picture she had up on the screen. It showed a picture of a column with metal on stone with its name and description underneath. He felt goose bumps erupt on his arms as he read the caption. Aloud, he whispered, "The weeping column?" Hearing Charlotte ask about such a thing was one thing; seeing evidence that such a thing existed and was referred to by an ancient alien was another.

"That's one of the names," she replied to him with a knowing look on her face. She took her phone back and handed it to her grandfather to show him what they were talking about. She looked at Grant. "Sound familiar?"

Grant nodded as he thought his goose bumps were getting bigger. He marveled how calm she seemed to be. "It does," he said after he had taken a deep breath. He studied her face. "How did you know to look there?"

She nodded toward the clockworks. "The Sentinel sent me a glimpse of a structure before he went back into the movement. I recognized it." She looked back at Grant, her face set and determined.

"How did he know we needed that information?" Grant muttered as he thought about it. "Also, how did he know about this particular place?"

Charlotte shrugged as she took her phone back from her grandfather. "Perhaps it is something that the Sentinels know about, but the other wraiths do not. Since he knew the great evil was on earth, he knew to reveal the next step that was needed to defeat it."

Weldon watched them as they talked. He was clearly lost on the details of the conversation since they hadn't had a chance to tell him what the Oracle had revealed. They quickly filled him in so he could catch up. After they were finished, he thought for a while. "What I'd like to know," he said after a few minutes, "was why the Sentinel wasn't able to capture the evil. Isn't that why they were created, to fight this same evil?"

Charlotte looked toward the tower clock mechanism. "If I had to guess, it was because he was not at his full strength after his ordeal. And the evil has become stronger because it has merged with humans," she said quietly as she turned back toward Grant and Weldon. "I have seen the enemy, and

I know we need something powerful to fight it. The Oracle pointed me in that direction." She looked at her phone again to study the picture for a few more moments. When she dropped the phone in her pocket, she faced Grant.

He met her eyes and saw that she was not scared or intimidated. He briefly caught a glimpse of a great inner power and strength he had not seen before. As he nodded to her, he wondered if he should be worried whether he was worthy enough for her. Setting those thoughts aside, he decided the enemy should worry more about tangling with her.

Weldon had pulled out his phone and was working rapidly as he tapped and swiped the screen several times. "Okay," he said as he read the screen, "tickets for Istanbul." He stopped and looked at them. They both turned to give him their full attention. "How many tickets do I order?" he asked as his eyes moved from one to the other.

Charlotte gazed up at Grant. Her face did not reveal any of her thoughts, but her expression was soft and curious. "I have one question."

"Yes?" he asked. He felt his insides tighten as he waited, unsure what she would be asking. He dared not hope too much or fear the worst.

"Do you have someone taking care of Gustav?"

He was momentarily confused as he thought, *Gustav, my cat?* He mentally wiped away the confusion to answer, "Yes, I called a pet sitter friend. She's checking on him a couple of times a day."

"I have another question." She tilted her head to smile at him mischievously.

"You said you only had one," Grant shot back. He was still tense, but he smiled at her.

"I thought of another," she said matter-of-factly. "It is just as important."

Grant raised his eyebrows questioningly and nodded for her to go ahead and ask.

"Who is watching the shop and did you deliver that grandfather clock to the sweet old man?"

Grants quirked a quick grin as he shook his head slightly in reaction to the queries. He wasn't going to bother to point out that she had asked two more questions. "The clock is delivered and the shop is closed. I put a note on the sign that if anyone needed me to call my cell phone."

She smiled at him. "Good! All bases are covered," she declared as she turned to Weldon. "Make that three. If," she looked back over her shoulder at him, "Grant wants to go."

Grant felt relief and hope wash over him. He grinned back at her happily and was going to answer when he heard Weldon say, "Three it is." Weldon looked up at Grant to meet his eyes and winked. He had known what Grant wanted.

Charlotte shook her head slightly at her men as she smiled at them with gentle affection.

CHAPTER TWENTY

After he had escaped, Carlos had run as fast as he could away from the warehouse. When he had covered several blocks in a sprint, he dared to look behind him to see no one chasing him. He slowed down to a fast walk as he considered his options. He knew his cover was blown and that he was now known amongst the other Keepers and their wraiths for what he was, the evil Keeper they had been looking for. He was also internationally known because of his position in the financial world. He pondered these facts and found he wasn't sure where he could hide. But overshadowing all these other thoughts was his concern about the essence of pure evil that had possessed him. He desperately needed to leave the area fast and hope that it couldn't find him.

When he couldn't contact his local gang of wraith bad boys, he knew that they had been trapped somehow. He didn't know how. There should have been nothing to seize his wraiths with the Sentinel weakened and the Time Keepers' vaults still disabled.

His panic was momentarily quelled with a prideful smirk. *The stupid Keepers,* he thought as he slowed his pace to stroll down the street. *They should've known the weakness of the vault's power conduit.* Although the intricate mechanism of cogs and gears that made up the vaults were spring driven, those huge springs had to be wound by a powerful source. Many of the Keepers used either geo- or solar-thermal energy to run the motors. But the link between these sources and the springs were vulnerable. Carlos had exploited this weakness by planting a device within this link when he volunteered to be part of the team to run maintenance on all of the Keepers' vaults decades prior. Each mini-bomb was susceptible to a specific frequency burst that caused it to explode with an intensity that would warp the springs. The delivery system for the pulse was an orbiting satellite around Earth that he owned. When he had triggered it to deliver the pulse, it resonated through the atmosphere and shutdown the vaults, just as he had planned years ago.

He smirked again as he spotted a perfect place to regroup. "Stupid Keepers," he muttered as he stopped to glance behind himself to make sure he still wasn't followed. "Your lot never made sure your vaults were still plugged in!"

He slipped inside the battered wooden doorway into a rundown, seedy hotel. After he had paid the desk attendant for a room for twenty-four hours, he had the key and directions to his new hiding place. He gingerly walked up the dimly lit, rickety stairs to the third floor and into a shabby room.

After he closed the door behind him, he stifled a shudder as he looked around the tired and dreary room. It was sparsely furnished with a bed and single wooden chair. The blinds on the single window were drawn all the way up but splintered pieces hung down randomly like broken teeth. He could imagine the vermin that called this place their home and thought he could hear the skittering sounds of tiny claws and muted squeaks in the mildewed stained walls.

He pushed those thoughts out of his mind as he sat down gingerly on the rickety wooden chair. It was the only piece of furniture in the room he trusted as he avoided the questionable bed with its tattered linens. Trying not to breathe the musty and soured air in too deeply, he pulled out his mobile and focused on contacting the members of his syndication. He was overdue in updating them.

After sending a group text, he sat back to wait for replies. He impatiently tapped at the arm of the chair as he stared at his screen. As the minutes ticked by, he became angry and nervous. The people he had pulled into his scheme were social outcasts and misfits. They were nervous and flighty. He worried that since he had missed his appointed time to contact them, they may have scattered like birds being hunted by a dog.

His brewing thoughts were interrupted as he felt an icy shudder crawl up his spine. He suddenly sensed a cold, evil presence nearby. Startled, he kicked the chair over as he jumped out of it to look around the room. As he turned slowly, he saw the ugly, green-black miasma ooze into the room through a black mold stain on the ceiling. Sheer panic took over as he threw down his mobile and tried to run. His only thought was the electric need to avoid being possessed by that pure evil entity again.

He wildly looked around the room, seeking escape. At first, he started to run out the door into the hall but was blocked by the rapidly expanding and contracting cloud. Pure fear enveloped him as he ran and circled around the room as the presence stalked him relentlessly.

Blinded by terror, he jumped out through the closed window with a loud crashing crack of dirty, old glass. Without a shout or cry, he fell three stories, smashed through the branches of an old tree, and ended with a solid thud on the hard ground. His crumpled body testified to his lifeless state. He had achieved what he sought; he could no longer be possessed.

When a contingent of bad wraiths from the surrounding areas came to investigate their Keeper's body, they milled around in confusion at the sight of the death of a Time Keeper. This was something they had not witnessed in centuries because of the clockworks rooms that extended their human companions' lives. In this state of uncertainty, they were surprised and quickly overwhelmed by the evil entity that had waited in ambush for them.

After they were totally possessed, they regrouped, and with a single mind directing them, it decided their course of action for them. With their evil tendencies enhanced, it urged them to seek out whoever remained of their ilk. Its plan was to use any wraith it could possess to wage a final battle against all the wraiths that opposed it and their human Keepers.

Very quickly, the evil entity found that it was not satisfied with the group of wraiths it possessed. It sought others throughout England. Even after it expanded its collection of evil and unwary wraiths, it still wasn't satiated. It had grown too powerful while it possessed a human. It had to seek out a human host. It was hungry for someone with power who could wreak its revenge against the remnant of Society that had survived and thrived on this planet.

As it contemplated the humans it had encountered, it focused on one. The one that had the attentions and affections of its last host. It hungered to find and possess the Chosen One. The entity was filled with evil glee as it thought how perfect it would be to destroy the wraiths by the one who was supposed to save them.

CHAPTER TWENTY-ONE

Becker sped to her destination. She hated to leave so soon after the events at the warehouse, but the latest news she had gotten from those guarding the pocket watches had her worried. The newcomers were emerging from the watches. She had seen that Grant, Charlotte, and Weldon were safe and guarded at their London hotel before she had left. They were leaving for Istanbul the next morning, and she needed to get to the States and back before then. With an extra burst of speed, she arrived at Weldon's mansion within minutes.

She joined the group of wraiths hovering near the table where the watches of different sizes, styles, and composition were laid out. She could see the wispy forms coming out of the small timepieces to slowly take shape.

When they all emerged, they hovered over the table as they looked around an environment alien to them. Becker felt the guards react when they recognized whom they had been guarding. She was not surprised. She had suspected who they had been and the Oracle had confirmed it.

Becker slowly moved in closer to greet the Royals, the ruling family of their Society. They had been the last to leave their home in space, and no one knew until now that they had survived. Becker drew in even nearer and bowed to a pair of wraiths that were half again larger than she was.

"Zaranethia, what has happened while we were separated?" the king asked her.

Becker hesitated. She hadn't heard her given name or her native language in so long it took her time to understand. "Much, my liege," she answered before the royal couple grew too restless with waiting.

"How long has it been?" the queen asked.

"On this planet, many of their centuries have passed," Becker answered more quickly.

"How are our people?" the queen asked.

"We have lived peacefully side by side with humans. Most are in communities, some loners."

"How about the trouble makers?" the king asked as he looked around and studied the other wraiths with them.

"The humans had them imprisoned until recently when a bad one of their kind disabled their means. But the Sentinels were activated to handle that."

"I see." The king looked around and stared at the doorway to the dining area. "So how are the humans as hosts?" he asked as he saw the butler come into the room to wind the pocket watches. "It looks as if within them is the force and rhythm of life." He started to move closer to the human.

"Sire," Becker reached out to stop him from reaching the unsuspecting man.

"How dare you attempt to command me!" The king wheeled around and pulled free from her grasp. He lashed out at her but was too weak to cause her any harm.

The rest of the wraiths that had been guarding the watches circled him to protect Winston.

"Sire, that is not done," Becker insisted. She tried to remain calm in the face of his fury. She silently thanked the

Power Above All that his power had not yet reemerged or she would've been destroyed.

"Our source of nourishment is no longer available to us. It seems we have been traveling through eternity without sustenance. His heartbeat is strong. I need nourishment," the king started to rage.

Several others of the royal family started to move toward Winston.

"No!" Becker shouted. They stopped in shock as they stared at her.

"You have no authority over us," one of them yelled at her. "We must survive! We are royalty!"

With a gesture, Becker commanded the wraiths who had been guards to disperse and grab each one of the newcomers. She had feared this reaction and had warned the guards of the possibility that they would need to apprehend the wraiths after they had emerged. She hadn't told them who she suspected they were and was proud that they did not hesitate to follow her commands even though they now knew it was the Royals they were dealing with.

The queen watched quietly. She hadn't moved at all. She was obviously stunned by her family's actions or by the response of the wraiths to her family. She gestured to get Becker's attention. "Zaranethia, you have been a faithful protector of this family and a friend." She moved to hover near her. "Why are you turning against us?"

Becker ducked her head in a bow. "With respect, my queen, we have been without rulers and have lived amongst a race where the majority of them have lived in democracies. Our Society has changed to adjust to this world."

"I see," the queen muttered as she thought about what she was told. "We were gone for far too long." She looked at her family and the way they were acting as they fought against those that firmly held them. After a few minutes, she turned back to face Becker. "But there is something more, isn't there?"

Becker waved her away from the others to talk with her more privately. "The great evil is suspected to have come here with you and your family."

The queen was shocked, then angry. "What are you saying? What are you accusing us of?" Her anger suddenly built into a raging fury.

Becker looked at her in shock, then sighed. "You have been touched by the evil," she whispered sadly. She gestured to a pair of wraiths who did not yet have a captive. They immediately came forward to restrain the queen.

As sadness filled her being, Becker stood apart from them so she could look at each one of the newcomers. As she contemplated the situation, Ansonia glided over to her.

"What do you think?" he asked quietly. Becker could tell he was also upset by the unfolding situation.

"I don't sense the great evil being present," she said quietly to him. "But either the long time in space has affected them, or the great evil had been in their midst and left its mark."

Ansonia nodded sadly as he looked at the restrained royal family. "It is a shame; they could help."

Becker nodded. "Yes, they could have. They are more powerful in their abilities than we are. From the way they are acting right now, they cannot be trusted. They will do more damage to the humans than we ever could."

"Agreed." Ansonia nodded then went to talk to the wraiths guarding the royals.

Becker watched Winston winding the watches. He had faithfully kept them running for beings he couldn't sense or see. She didn't know how to tell him that he didn't need to do it any longer.

She looked away from the human to nod at the guards that were waiting for her command. "Take them to the designated clocks we have prepared. Keep them secure."

As the group moved to take away the royals, Becker muttered, "I am sorry, my queen, my friend. This is how it needs to be for now."

Before she left, she scanned all the watches to make sure no one was left. They were all empty. She was about to leave when a wraith came floating in.

"Hey, where is everyone?" he asked. "Did I miss the party?"

Becker smiled at how he sounded so much like his Keeper. "Hi, Max," she greeted him. She still found the name he had been given to be funny sounding. But he had been named by John, Grant's friend and fellow Keeper. "They emerged and were escorted to their clocks."

"Ah," the wraith said as he looked at Winston, still winding the pocket watches. "Guess he doesn't know it."

Becker shook her head. "No one around that can tell him."

"Was it the royals?" Max asked.

"Yes," she said sadly. Then she looked at him sharply. "How did you know?" she asked, intensely curious.

He shrugged in response. "Lucky guess. Nothing had been heard about them at all over the centuries." Max looked at her hard. "Shouldn't it be good that they survived?"

Becker met his eyes. "Yes, I am glad they survived. But the Society has changed because of the fact that we have been living with humans."

"True," Max agreed, his face sobering as he thought. "They don't expect to pick up rule where they left off?"

"I believe they do," Becker nodded. She kept her eyes downcast.

"Is there something else?" Max asked suspiciously.

"They have been touched by the great evil," she stated simply.

Max's face fell. "Not good," he said gravely. "The great evil is definitely here then."

Becker nodded. "I encountered it in London."

"I heard the Chosen One is okay," Max replied cheerfully as he changed the subject quickly.

Becker smiled and nodded. She knew he preferred more upbeat conversations and was glad for the subject change. "She is well." Nothing could be done about the royals being tainted at that moment. All she could do was hope and pray to the Power Above All that there was a solution somehow.

"Good," Max nodded. He looked at Winston again and then back at Becker. "I'm going to head back and update John. He hadn't been able to contact Grant and was worried."

"He's fine," she said quickly. Her face tensed as her mind jumped to the next challenge they all faced.

Max could see that she was worried and deep in thought. "Is there anything I can do to help?" he asked when he noticed that she was distracted.

Becker studied him. "Well, if you could have John contact Winston and let him know he can put away his watches. That would be good."

Max nodded. "Anything else?" he gently pushed.

"I need to secure the royals better. When they regain full strength, we won't be able to hold them. They will ruin this world."

Max nodded. He knew the power the royals possessed. Crossing his skeletal arms across his chest as he hovered, he bowed his head. "That is heavy, dude. Heavy." He thought awhile. "What about those silver cubes?"

Becker looked at him in interest. "What do you mean?"

"They trap our kind in the clockworks, right?"

"True. That is true," she muttered. "I don't know why I hadn't thought of that." She felt like kicking herself since she had personally experienced being trapped in her own clock by one of those cubes when she was kidnapped. And more recently, Grant had used them to corral the bad wraiths in London. Nodding to herself, she met his eyes. "Can John tell Winston where they are so he can set those around the clocks the royals are in? And make sure to use all that are available. They will need many more to keep them trapped."

Max thought a moment. "He has some of them with him. With the ones your Keeper kept, that may be enough. I am sure he'll make a personal appearance to make sure it's done." He turned to leave. "I will tell him."

"Thanks," Becker said as he slipped through the walls to head home.

Becker contacted Ansonia and updated him on Max's visit. As she waited for him to answer, she looked through all the rooms in the mansion then circled the grounds. She felt that everything was secure for the time being. Once Ansonia confirmed that he received her update, she sped back across the ocean to meet her Keeper and the Chosen One at the hotel.

CHAPTER TWENTY-TWO

Soon after Becker had left to check on things back in America, Grant, Charlotte, and Winston agreed they needed to relax before their trip to Istanbul the next morning. They decided not to leave the hotel and arranged for room service. This did not discourage the local Keepers as they dropped by to visit with them under the guise of discussing what to do next about the escaped evil Keeper and the green-black cloud they had seen. Through all the discussions, it was clear to Grant and Winston that they studied the only female amongst them. It was obvious their main purpose was to check and make sure Charlotte was doing okay.

As the night grew late, they all politely said their goodnights and left the three alone to rest. After they ate their meal and the dishes had been picked up, Grant and Weldon decided to sit back and watch television. As they flipped through the channels, Grant muttered, "I wonder if there's a rerun of Midsomer Murders or Father Brown."

Weldon nodded, "I like those, too. There are quite a few shows I like to watch that are made in other countries."

"Do you like Murdock Mysteries?" Grant asked as he continued to look for something to watch.

"Ah, yes," Weldon smiled. "Canadian made. Love it."

Charlotte yawned as she watched her men investigate British television. She was bone weary. "I'm going to take a shower and go to bed."

Both of the men smiled and nodded at her as they said their goodnights.

After she pulled her sleep shirt from her luggage and gathered together her toiletries, she started the shower. As she adjusted the temperature, the steam rose around her like a comforting cloud. Breathing deeply, she allowed the steam to clear her mind as she started to relax. She hadn't realized until then how tense she was. She slipped into the shower and allowed the water to simply flow over her. Imagining the flow of water washing her thoughts, she emptied her mind of all the swirling memories of what had happened and of the present concerns of what might be in their near future.

As she enjoyed the sensation of the hot water loosening her tight and knotted muscles, the steam continued to thicken in the space around her. When she leaned back to let the water sluice over her scalp and down through her hair, she closed her eyes and smiled. She reached over to grab the shampoo to start washing her hair when she snatched her hand back and looked around warily. She had been suddenly struck by a feeling of wrongness. That's when she saw that she was being watched.

Intermingled with the steam of the shower was a group of wraiths that hovered around her. She quickly grabbed the shower curtain to wrap around herself. She knew these were not the type of wraiths she had been associating with; those wraiths were much too polite to do what these were doing. Plus, she sensed the sickening presence of intense evil.

After she yanked down the rod holding up the shower curtain, she pulled it off to keep herself covered as she backed out of the tub. The wraiths followed her as she moved out of the bathroom into her room. She wondered where her wraith companions were and how these evil ones had slipped through. She intended to shout for help and flee. Before she could open her mouth to cry out, a sickly green cloud of evil oozed out of the group of the dark, smoky beings and congealed together to attack her.

Her first instinct was to roll up like a ball, shut her eyes, and clamp her mouth shut. She mentally closed herself off as the evil buffeted her from every side as it tried to gain access to her innermost being.

She quickly discovered that a purely defensive posture sorely lacked strength against the evil entity. It patiently pulled down her defenses as it stuck sickly probes into her mind and soul. As its influence ignited fear, her defenses crumbled even more quickly as she reacted to the overpowering feeling of terror and panicked. Once she realized the full ramifications of her mistake, she regretted that she hadn't taken an active stance to fight it off. As she felt her body being taken over by the evil entity, all she could do was pray for help and for it to come quickly.

The men rushed into her room to check on her when they heard the crash of the shower curtain rod. As they stood in open-mouthed shock at what they saw, she slowly stood up from the floor as evil waves pulsed from her. As her rigid body turned stiffly toward them, her blazing, sickly green eyes leveled at Grant and Weldon as they stood frozen in place.

Charlotte was aware of her body's movements but couldn't do anything to stop it as the evil presence made her stand and point at her men threateningly. The cruel, harsh voice that emanated from her mouth made her shudder in the inner compartment of herself where she was forced to stay. "I will destroy you and every one of your kind," the evil entity sneered at them. "And I will destroy the rest of the Society!" It made her stalk toward them, hunched over and twisted, the very essence of looking demented. "It mocked me and refused to let me rule. If I cannot command it, it must be destroyed!" The words ended in an inhuman screech.

Grant and Weldon stared at the apparition in front of them. A female, barely recognizable as Charlotte, stalked them as water dripped on the floor from her soaking wet body. She was able to keep herself modestly covered by holding the opaque shower curtain in one hand. A dark green aura surrounded her as her eyes blazed with evil green intensity. The wraiths who had been left as guards came into the room to hover in indecision as they surrounded the three of them. The evil wraiths had fled, wanting nothing to do with an evil greater than themselves.

Even with the shock of seeing Charlotte in this horrific state, Grant was quicker to assess the situation since he had seen this same evil ooze out of Carlos at the warehouse. As he battled the intense mental and emotional turmoil of seeing one whom he loved being abused, he mentally ordered the wraiths to stay away. He worried that they would be possessed by this evil and reasoned that if a Sentinel couldn't defeat this presence, they surely couldn't. He also waved Weldon off, not willing to risk the evil touching the older man. He wanted to protect all he cared about, including Charlotte, who to all intents and purposes was being used by his enemy.

As Charlotte's body lurched toward him, evil twisting her lovely face and causing drool to drip from her mouth, his first instinct was to run. Instead, he steeled himself and forced himself to walk toward her, step by step, until they stood face to face. The nearness of the evil presence sickened him, causing him to want to double over in pain and despair. He forced himself to fight those feelings and was determined to stand his ground.

He felt fear try to overtake and control him as the dull green cloud reached out probing tendrils to encompass him. He closed his eyes and clamped his mouth. He was going to try to ride it through by staying on the defense. Suddenly he heard Charlotte's voice through the mental roar of the influence of the evil. The connection left by their encounter with the Sentinel was still there. All he could hear in his mind was her saying one word, *Offense.*

As he continued to try to block the evil, he pondered the word. As the entity broke down his defenses, little by little, he suddenly understood. His mind flurried like a dove avoiding a hawk as it sought a weapon. *Opposite of fear,* he thought. *Faith! What makes up faith*? He struggled to think through the mental turbulence the evil being caused. He stubbornly probed his own mind and all his experiences through centuries of life, hope, and love.

Hope! Love! He latched onto these concepts. Once he followed these to their roots of divine sacrifice, he found his offensive strategy. With these weapons, he drew on strength from his innermost being and flung off the shrouds and bonds that evil had enveloped him in. Once free, he reached through the miasma that surrounded Charlotte and grabbed her shower-curtain-draped body to pull her close. As he hugged her, he mentally linked with her again to share what he found.

He knew she understood when he felt her gather strength from the same core as he did and tap the power he had seen in her before. As he held onto her tightly, he felt the evil attacking them as it redoubled its efforts, causing them deep bodily and mental pain. He hung on to her, willing to sacrifice himself for her if needed.

When the time was right and she was strengthened enough, they stepped away from each other to turn to face the enemy. With hope and love forged as weapons in their thoughts and hearts, they drove the entity back. It reacted by shuddering violently and quickly drew its tendrils away from them like a hand away from a hot plate. It screeched horrifically in anger, pain, and terror as it withdrew but didn't flee.

Free of the entity, Grant wrapped the shower curtain more securely around Charlotte. When he saw that she had started to shake with cold and profound weakness from the encounter, he wrapped an arm around her. With her secure against him, he faced the green miasma that hovered and brooded. Lifting an arm to point at it, Grant stared at it and found he no longer feared it. "We know how to fight you," he declared loudly and firmly. "Try it again and you will suffer even more!"

The miasma swiftly moved toward them as if to attack them. But as they stood firmly together in defiance with all their being filled with hope and love, it diverted quickly and disappeared through the ceiling.

As soon as it was gone, they both heaved a great sigh of relief. With gentle care, Grant helped Charlotte to her bed. Weldon and their wraiths rushed toward them. None of them had left the room as they had been ordered to. They had been unwilling to leave the two to their fates with the evil entity.

"How did it get by the guards?!" Weldon was shaken and angry. He shot an accusing look at the hovering wispy, black beings. They looked embarrassed but stood their ground.

Grant held Charlotte after wrapping blankets snuggly around her shivering form over the shower curtain. "Wraiths have always been very polite and cautious about situations that we consider private," he explained to Weldon.

Weldon sighed deeply as he closed his eyes. After he controlled his anger, he stepped toward the bed to check on his granddaughter. "Are you okay?" He looked her over, then hugged her.

"Now I am," she smiled through chattering teeth. "They surprised me. I was enjoying the shower, then suddenly they were there, leering at me through the steam. It was the evil wraiths that brought the entity."

"More than one?" Weldon asked as he brought a nearby cushioned chair closer and sat down on it.

Grant held her closer. "Apparently, the evil wraiths, especially ones that were possessed, don't have the scruples of our wraiths," he muttered angrily as he thought of how she was attacked when she was the most vulnerable.

She nodded thoughtfully. "It came out of all of them. It was a huge group. It was like one of them couldn't contain it." Her voice was becoming steadier and stronger. Grant loosened his hold when her shivering stopped, but he didn't withdraw. She leaned against him gratefully.

"In other words, you think it's getting even stronger than when we saw it in the warehouse?" Weldon asked Grant as he met his eyes.

"I don't know for sure," Grant answered truthfully. He looked down at Charlotte. "There seems to be evidence that it is."

Weldon looked off into space as he thought for a while. Grant turned his full attention on Charlotte to make sure she was okay. He smoothed back the wet hair from her face as she looked up at him. Their deep contemplation of each other was broken when Weldon spoke again.

"This all seemed to happen about the time the newcomers came," he said thoughtfully. He looked from one to the other. "Do you think that there is a link, or is it coincidence?"

Grant thought about it as he rubbed his chin with his free hand. The more he thought, the more he could see connections, but he could also see holes. "I'm not sure," he said after a while. "Since Carlos had already been in action with his first plan of world domination before the last group of wraiths showed up, it could be coincidence." He thought further. "But if the bad wraiths were behind that original plan, could they have been influenced by the evil entity as it drew closer to the earth? Assuming it was brought here by the last group."

Weldon nodded as he followed Grant's train of thought. "Either theory could be true. One thing I know, it is able to fully possess and control wraiths and humans alike. What else can it do?"

Charlotte interrupted their thoughts when she moved away from Grant to unwrap the blankets he had tucked around her. She was warm and strong enough now to finish her shower. "All that may be true," she added matter-of-factly as she moved. "However, the point is, it is here, and we have to defeat it." She grabbed her bathrobe and slipped it on under the shower curtain. "And that is not happening right now," she added. Once she was clothed, she held out the shower curtain and looked at the men. "Could one of you rehang this so I can finish my shower?"

CHAPTER TWENTY-THREE

When Becker got back to London, she found out what had happened while she was gone. Although she was furious at the wraiths she had left to guard them, she couldn't chastise them too much. There was a strong and set rule amongst them about the privacy of humans. Also, she could see the impact of this invasion on her people. They were stricken by how impotent they had felt in the face of the evil entity.

When Becker communicated with Charlotte, she found that a large group of bad wraiths were involved. That worried her. She knew the evil had found its way to earth through at least one wraith; now it seemed to need more to possess. She thought of its possession of the evil Keeper. *That must have helped it strengthen and grow,* she thought to herself as she reviewed the facts. *Human evil strengthening wraith evil.* She was glad her humans found ways to fight it off, but she knew it needed to be destroyed before it got even stronger and destroyed them all.

Her thoughts went back to the evil Keeper. *What happened to him,* she thought suddenly, *to make the entity seek another host?* She called to her team and sent them out with the mission to find Carlos.

The wraiths she sent out soon enlisted the help of the local wraiths for a quicker search. In no time, they had gotten word to meet the other wraiths near a shabby building that looked as if it were fit for demolition. Under the broken branches of an old tree, they found the dead body of Carlos.

The humans had also found him, as the area was swarming with police officials investigating the death.

The wraiths noted the broken window on the third floor and the broken branches starting from that point down. After they accessed the room through the broken window, they found the evil Keeper's mobile. After examining the room further and not finding anything else, they contacted Becker.

Becker sped over to the scene to look it over for herself. She couldn't tell if he had been pushed or jumped, but he was now out of the picture. She had one of the local wraiths contact any Keeper in the police force to examine the mobile. She knew Carlos had other people working with him in his first attempt at world domination and figured he was still in touch with them. She worried that whoever they were could become hosts or even had wraiths who worked in conjunction with them that may be able hosts for the entity.

When Becker caught up with Charlotte, Grant, and Weldon, they were already on board a jet heading for Istanbul. She showed them images of what happened to Carlos. When she was done, they looked at each other in concern.

Weldon was the first to whisper, "I don't know if this is good or bad news."

Grant sat back in the airline seat, rubbing his chin. He was deep in thought. "I wonder if that was why the entity attacked Charlotte," he said as he looked at the others. "I wonder where it went."

Charlotte looked from her grandfather to him. "I am sure we will find the entity soon enough. As far as Carlos is concerned, we don't know who else was working with him." She shook her head slightly. "We don't know if he had any other plan in action."

"Becker indicated she had police look into his phone. Any Keeper on the force can follow up in that regard," Grant commented.

"His network may fall apart now that it is leaderless," Weldon said hopefully.

Grant shifted slightly in his seat and looked from one to the other. "Or someone else will take over." He turned to Charlotte. "What will happen if that evil thing stays to inhabit just the wraiths? What if it gets powerful enough to simply take over every wraith on earth?"

She looked away as the image of a previous vision enveloped her. "It will be worse than last time. Their society that they have built here over the centuries will tear itself apart," she whispered hoarsely.

Becker nodded sadly as she floated over them. When she saw Charlotte looking up at her, she made a gesture with her hands and arms.

"What did that mean?" Grant asked. He didn't like the looks of the motion the wraith had made.

Charlotte's eyes started tearing up. Before she answered, she took a deep, shuddering breath. "That is their signal for annihilation."

"Annihilation?" Weldon repeated in surprise. His grey, bushy eyebrows rose up, nearly meeting his hairline.

"Yes," Charlotte ducked her head and swallowed as she tried to keep from crying. The image of the destruction of the previous Society flashed again in her mind and expanded, showing even further destruction and chaos. "This is the final battlefield."

Grant and Weldon looked in horror at Charlotte, then up at Becker, who was nodding sadly.

"And the impact on mankind?" Weldon asked tensely in a hoarse whisper.

Charlotte looked at Becker, then out the window. "A greater evil presence is in our world. Combine that with an alien evil force that could further affect memories and time perception..." She hesitated as she turned back to look from Weldon to Grant. "...could very well destroy our world as well."

Grant looked up at Becker. He suddenly had a question that he had never thought to ask before. He tried to mentally ask her, but her answer didn't make sense to him.

Charlotte creased her brow as she watched them. "What are you trying to find out from her?" she asked curiously.

"We've always thought the wraiths came to earth because of the rhythm of the human heart."

Weldon nodded. "Isn't that why they can exist in clockworks, because of the similar rhythm?"

Grant nodded at him, then faced Charlotte. "But what if there is something else they need from us. And they were escaping the evil to find it. Something the evil doesn't want them to find."

Charlotte nodded as she followed his train of thought. "The Oracle..." she started to say, then stopped to organize her thoughts. "The post that weeps – no – the orb of hope." She stared up at Becker, who was watching them talk and seemed to be waiting for something. "There is more than the sound of the human heart, isn't there?"

Becker nodded solemnly. She didn't offer the Keepers any insights. She simply hovered and waited.

"I guess we're going to have to figure that out," Charlotte said as she looked away.

Suddenly Becker looked around and became very worried. Within moments, she sped out of the plane. All three Keepers looked around to see what could've triggered her reaction.

Charlotte looked out of the jet's window to see a cloud of wraiths surrounding the plane. Within seconds, another group sped toward them to violently clash together in battle.

"Hold on," she shouted to everyone. Suddenly, the plane bucked and dropped. The overhead seatbelt sign flashed on. The pilot's voice announced turbulence over the intercom.

"We're being attacked," Charlotte whispered to Grant and Weldon. They both looked over her to peer outside the window.

"If we don't safeguard the pilot and copilot, the plane is doomed." Grant muttered as he looked around. He saw no wraiths in the cabin yet.

"Can Becker and her group fight them off?" Weldon leaned over Grant to ask Charlotte. He didn't want the other passengers to hear him.

She watched the action from her window. "Looks equally matched from what I can see."

"Doesn't mean that one won't slip through," Grant whispered as he rubbed his chin. "Anyone have any cubes handy? Mine are in my suitcase."

Charlotte reached down to her purse under her seat. She reached in and pulled out a handful. "Some from our warehouse incident," she whispered as she handed them to her grandfather.

"How did you get those by security?" Weldon asked as he took them from her.

"They didn't seem to notice them," she shrugged. "Thought they were toys, I guess."

Without saying a word, Weldon slipped out into the aisle, bracing against seats as the plane continued to buck and drop.

"Sir!" one of the attendants shouted at him from the seat she was buckled into. "You need to get back to your seat and buckle up!"

He made his way over to her seat. Once there, despite the rocking and bucking of the plane, he bent down to whisper to her. After he was finished, she looked at him with wide eyes and nodded. After he whispered to her again, she nodded again, then unbuckled.

Suddenly the jet started to nose dive. Everyone screamed and panicked as they scrambled to grab hold of something to hang onto.

Grant, worried that they were running out of time, was going to slip out of his seat to help Weldon, when Charlotte stopped him. He glanced at her, then looked to see what she was drawing his attention toward. She was nervously watching her grandfather as he and the stewardess were making their way to the pilots. Grant relaxed as best he could as he leaned back into the seat and held on.

The stewardess spoke to the pilot through the door. Soon the copilot opened the door and let them in. Within seconds, the plane leveled out and flew without any further problems.

After a few minutes, Weldon emerged from the cockpit and made his way back to his seat empty handed.

Charlotte looked out the window. The battle still raged but the plane seemed safe.

Weldon sat down with a tired sigh. Before they could ask, he whispered. "One, just one, wraith had gotten in the cockpit. He was having a hey day going from one crewmember to the other."

Charlotte leaned over Grant to whisper, "How did you get the stewardess to help you into the cabin?"

Weldon smiled, then looked sheepish. "I told her I was a secret agent and we were being attacked by an ultra-secret weapon."

Charlotte and Grant smiled at his quick thinking. "So the cubes were a way to neutralize this weapon?" Grant filled in.

Weldon nodded.

"Brilliant!" Grant smiled, then sobered as he saw a wraith coming into the cabin.

Charlotte looked out the window. She couldn't see any wraiths at all anywhere around the plane as far as she could see.

"It's Becker," Grant whispered to her. "She's reporting."

After she was done, Grant rubbed his eyes. "Rogue wraiths. No Keeper. They are organizing without human intervention. Becker says the great evil inhabits them. The bad boys are now worse."

"I wonder if any Sentinel can capture them now," Charlotte worried as she thought of the potential result of the enhancement of evil.

"Becker is leaving her team to watch over us," Grant said. "She has to go and meet with other leaders."

Charlotte nodded to Becker. She wondered why she hadn't relayed the information to her as well. She mentally asked her, but the wraith smiled and shrugged. "You're holding something back," she telepathically accused the wispy being.

Becker responded to her, "You need to find out the pieces to the puzzle on your own."

"You know?!" Charlotte wasn't sure which surprised her more, the realization that there were deeper secrets to the wraiths, or that Becker spoke to her in words.

"Not all. Some. But I may steer you wrong. Best to continue your path of discovery." With that said, Becker sped away.

CHAPTER TWENTY-FOUR

After the evil entity tried to possess Charlotte and after it was prevented from bringing down the jet she traveled in, it had to break off from the hunt to find a better host. Inhabiting a multitude of wraiths could no longer satisfy its needs. It had to find another human host. It hungered and ached for the alien human fears, depression, and hopelessness that strengthened and intensified its nature. Finding a willing human whose basic character was bad would not only be in sync with its evil nature, it would be an even better host.

The entity had been born out of the wraiths' evil deeds and desires, but now it had evolved and adapted to feed off the dark side of human souls. It was aware that it was no match for the evil that already existed in the human world and psyche. It counted on either ingratiating itself to this resident presence to increase the intensity of evil on this planet or to somehow survive in its shadow and thrive.

As it brooded on its existence, it recalled memories that it had encountered in Charlotte's mind. It took notice of one she remembered as Curtis. It noted that her recollections about this human were colored with worry and fear. With this information, it decided to drive the group of evil wraiths it possessed to seek out this human.

* * * * * * *

Curtis had been waiting impatiently for the secret signal from Carlos. He didn't understand why he hadn't heard anything since it was well beyond the expected time limit. As he thought about Carlos, his mind wandered back to part of his memory he had been fighting to regain.

He didn't know what had happened on the roof the day of the wraith battle. He couldn't remember anything that happened in the huge black gap that he saw when he looked back. All he could remember was running out of the store where Carlos had stationed him with the controller. He was to monitor the battle and command the wraiths under their control to fight with the evil wraiths against the wraiths of the Keepers.

He had spent months trying to piece together from his Swiss cheese memory how it came to the point that he saw a huge being that looked to be made up of black smoke and sand. Although the images he had seen on the controller were simple renditions of figures that didn't reveal their true appearance, he knew from Charlotte's descriptions from when they were kids that it was a Time Wraith he had seen. What puzzled him was that she had never described them as being huge.

He paced the padded room as he demanded more information from his mind. His last outburst, fueled by impatience, had landed him in solitary confinement. His mind was still groggy from the sedative they used to get him into the room. His arms, hands, legs, and feet hurt as he vaguely remembered fighting several people when he lost control. As he walked, his mind began to clear more so he could think.

He was still agitated but fought to control it so they wouldn't give him any more drugs. He knew something was wrong with the plan. "Carlos, where are you?" he whined as he slumped down into the corner of the room with his head clutched between his hands.

His mind drifted back to before the battle of the wraiths, to before all the preparations that had come to nothing. He thought of his first contact with a Time Keeper who was willing to talk and share about the mysterious world of the Time Wraiths. He had told Carlos that he had been surprised and angry that his sister had been seeing something that he couldn't.

Carlos had listened to him with a caring attitude, showing he understood his plight. Then he had nodded and smiled at him, making him feel welcome, while he drew him into his exclusive circle with charm and acceptance. He not only told Curtis what he knew of the alien beings but gave him a device so he could see the creatures.

The feeling of being part of a secret society thrilled Curtis to the core. So when he met Carlos in the dense fog of a London alley months ago, he was frightened, but excited at the same time, to receive the equipment needed to help them conquer the world with the help of the wraiths.

His face fell as he remembered when Carlos found out more details about his sister. He was so jealous that his friend wanted to know everything he could tell him about her. After that, Carlos focused on his sister and barely gave him any thought. He wasn't sure why, but the fact that his sister got all the attention bothered him.

As he sat in the padded room, these thoughts stirred his internal torment to a boiling point. Soon it manifested physically as he started to bang the back of his head against the padded walls and hit the floor with his fists. He knew, he just knew, Carlos was with his sister and never wanted to see him again! *He doesn't need me anymore!* he thought in anguish. *The secret society abandoned me. I am nothing! Nothing! Again!*

He barely heard the door open and the soft footsteps of many cushioned shoes. He hardly registered the prick of the needle as he fought his internal demons. He was in mid-howl when the drugs kicked in and he passed out.

CHAPTER TWENTY-FIVE

"Master Gregory," the doctor spoke with a firm but kind tone. "Curtis has grown especially agitated of late."

"What has happened?" Worry and confusion was relayed over the phone connection. "I thought he was stable and responding to treatment."

"He was," the doctor agreed. He sighed heavily. He had to give particulars that he knew the patient's family did not want to hear. "He became suddenly violent." He paused to let it sink in. When no questions were asked, he continued hoping that he hadn't lost connection. He knew Master Gregory was in Europe and worried about relaying bad news over phone connections he knew could be unstable. "He hurt several of the attendants." He was going to continue when he heard a response.

"Are they okay?" Weldon asked quietly. His voice registered true concern for whomever his grandson hurt.

"They will be okay. Two of them had to be hospitalized because he beat them badly. But nothing that will permanently affect them." The doctor winced as he moved his splinted arm. "We were able to sedate him and place him in a padded room before he could hurt himself."

"I see," the voice replied. "Did he say anything that may point to the reason for this change in him?"

The doctor thought wearily. He needed another dose of pain medicine soon, but he hadn't wanted to take it before he could contact the family. "I'm not sure." He paused as he replayed the violent scene back over in his mind. "He was screaming and shouting. The words were hard to make out. I think he said something about 'Carloo,' 'Cartlus,' or something." He rubbed his face with his unbound hand as he thought.

"Could it have been 'Carlos'?" the elder man's voice asked quietly.

"Yes, that's it!" the doctor confirmed. "Yes, something about not contacting him or something." He stopped as he thought. "Do you have a family member named Carlos?"

"No." The voice sounded distant. The speaker was already moving on to something else. "Thank you, doctor. Keep us updated on his condition."

"Yes, sir," the doctor responded before he realized the connection was already broken. He looked at his phone curiously, then sighed and shrugged. He hurt too much to try to figure out the reaction of Curtis's grandfather. Popping pain pills, he lay down, thankful he was at home and could mend during his sick leave.

Even if he hadn't passed out, he still wouldn't have seen the smoky cloud that appeared as it hovered near his ceiling. The group of wraiths had tracked the phone call to find the doctor sleeping in his recliner with his feet up, head back, and mouth wide open.

The doctor was blissfully unaware of the sinister miasma that oozed out of the cloud of wraiths and hovered over him. As it extended seeking tendrils to test the waters before possessing this unwary human, the wraiths tried to break and run. The entity fractured part of itself to send a piece into each one of the shadowy beings to hold them in place. It wasn't willing to lose its temporary hosts until it knew what its next step was.

Assured that its wraith victims were in hand, it turned its attention to the doctor. Very soon, it found in the doctor's thoughts and memories that he would not be seeing Curtis for a span of time. The entity changed its plan. Instead of using a human to find the other human for its host, it decided to find Curtis using the wraiths. It knew where it needed to go from the doctor's mind. Entering the group of wraiths again, it forced them to speed toward the hospital.

Seconds later, it was at the mental facility. It dispersed its imprisoned wraiths throughout the building, enabling it to search it more rapidly. Soon it found Curtis in the isolation room.

It pulled all the wraiths together as a group into the padded room. After the entity emerged from the wraiths, it hovered over the crumpled, heavily sedated body of a little man with dirty blonde hair that spiked out from his head in all directions. The partially viewed face sported a wisp of a beard that was wet with drool from a slack mouth. Even with sedation, Curtis' body twitched and his face twisted in maniacal fury.

The evil entity continued to hold the wraiths as before. It was unwilling to attempt to possess this individual without checking out the compatibility. It did not want to undergo the torment it had experienced before when it encountered the Chosen One and her companion. Sending out its tendrils, it tapped into the mind and psyche of Curtis. After finding a favorable environment, it quickly flowed into his body.

Curtis jerked violently once, then lay still. The wraiths were now free of any restraint and fled the building. Their master had a new host. They knew it could command them again at any moment, but right then they wanted a taste of freedom, no matter how short.

A few moments later, the attendants came to check on Curtis. Seeing he was sedated, they picked him up and strapped him onto a stretcher. Carrying him out of the padded room, they took him back to his own room. Within twenty-four hours, he had escaped.

* * * * * * *

"Master Gregory?" the female voice was familiar to Weldon. He knew she was the director of the mental health facility where Curtis resided. He was instantly on high alert since she only called when there was a huge problem.

"Yes, Amanda." He knew his voice sounded wary and harsh.

"Is this a good time?" she asked. Her voice quavered with nervousness.

Uh, oh, Weldon thought. *This is not good at all.* "Will it ever be a good time?" he asked as he gentled his voice but also clenched a fist as he braced himself. He sensed Charlotte and Grant watching him. He couldn't meet Charlotte's questioning eyes yet.

The female voice sighed heavily. She sounded like she was going to cry. "Curtis has escaped," she stated bluntly.

In the silence after the statement, Weldon was at first stunned speechless, then shocked with the implications. Then he wanted to know how. He took a deep breath and had to challenge all of his social skills to be civil. "And how did this happen?"

She had waited for him to ask. She stepped through events since the last contact they had with Weldon. "We were checking on him every ten minutes while he was sedated. Once he was awake, we checked on him every thirty minutes when he was restrained. When we felt he was calm enough to remove the restraints, we were going to check on him every hour. He went missing within the first hour." She paused as she waited for feedback from Weldon.

Weldon considered the facts that she had laid out carefully. "Any idea how he got out of a secure facility?"

"We think he stole a key card."

"Why has he never attempted that before?" he wondered out loud.

"We do not know." She paused as she picked her words carefully. "It was strange. When he came out of the sedation, he was different."

"In what way?"

"He was…" she hesitated, "…colder. More indifferent. More self-assured and calculating. Disassociated."

"Could it have been the sedation causing altered behavior?"

"No," the voice was sure. "It had been used on him before. Same dosing."

"I see," he said quietly while he looked at Grant and Charlotte. "What steps have been taken to find him?"

We have thoroughly searched the grounds. We also have contacted the authorities, and they are looking for him as well."

"I see." He noted that Grant, the wraith, had approached and was trying to get his attention. He pointed to Charlotte. "Keep me informed."

"Yes, sir," the voice was relieved that the call was at its end. "We are very sorry and concerned for his well-being."

"Thank you. I trust that there will be a review of this incident and implementation of a plan to prevent this from happening again?" he asked as he watched Charlotte. Her face had turned white while the wraith was communicating to her.

"Most assuredly," Amanda's voice had regained her firm confidence and sense of command.

"Good," he answered, then disconnected. He needed to hear the news that had upset his granddaughter so much. He had a feeling it was another report on his grandson Curtis. He met Grant's eyes, then glanced at the driver.

In the confines of the vehicle they were in, Weldon noted Grant looking from him to Charlotte. He was obviously confused about what was happening and sensed that something was very wrong.

They were in a cab that had been waiting for them at the airport in Istanbul and was heading toward their hotel. They were glad that a local Keeper had volunteered to be available for their travel needs while they were there. Being one of them, he knew that their purpose was important even though he wasn't aware of the details. Weldon glanced at the driver again. Even though he was a Keeper, he didn't think he should overhear the upcoming conversation. No one was sure if there were other Keepers who had been involved with Carlos and his plans.

"How long to the hotel?" Grant asked the driver.

"Not long," he answered in perfect English as he navigated an intersection.

Weldon glanced at his watch. Hugging Charlotte close, he met Grant's eyes. "We'll catch a quick bite after we get to the hotel. The other place is about to close. We need to relax anyway. We'll discuss things then."

Grant sat back in the seat. He was obviously frustrated that there was something going on and he was completely in the dark. Weldon saw him look to Grant, the wraith. Weldon didn't say anything as he watched as the wraith floated closer to him and started to communicate. Grant's expression changed as he received enough information to have a sense of what was going on.

Grant met his eyes and nodded, then looked out of the window. Weldon sighed to himself. *At least he got enough information to be satisfied for the time being,* he thought wearily. *We'll piece it all together once we have privacy.* He hugged Charlotte even closer as he also turned toward the window to watch the city flow by as the taxi sped through the streets of Istanbul.

CHAPTER TWENTY-SIX

Once they had gotten to their hotel room, Charlotte, Weldon, and Grant had an in-depth discussion about Curtis. With the information they had at hand, each voiced their concerns and speculations about what his escape could mean. When they had no additional facts to work with, all they could do was to accomplish what they had come to Turkey to do.

Becker had the wraiths looking for Curtis as soon as she had been notified, but by morning, she had nothing new to report to the Keepers. He seemed to have dropped off the face of the earth.

After a fitful night, they had nothing more to discuss about him the next day and concentrated on their mission.

They arrived at their destination as soon as it opened to the public. After their driver dropped them off, they faced the ancient building that had been a church, a mosque, and now a museum, the Hagia Sophia. Without any hesitation to admire the imposing edifice, they quickly made their way into the main part of the grand structure and soon stood at the weeping post, also known as the wishing column.

Even though the entire building was amazing with the intricacies of architecture and rich colors in the various symbols of Christian and Muslim faiths, Grant had his eyes on Charlotte. She had been acting strangely since they had landed in Turkey. He could tell that Weldon had noted it, too, but neither one of them had voiced his thoughts. They both knew that the last time she had looked so distracted and faraway, she had revealed detailed information about the Time Wraiths that had been previously unknown to the Keepers.

But he had to admit that, as they stood in front of the large stone column with a metal band that had a hole in it on one side, she was even more intense than ever. She paid no attention to the line of people that had already formed by the column to insert their thumb in the hole and rotate their hand clockwise before withdrawing it.

When the odd ritual had drawn his attention away from Charlotte for a few moments, Grant saw several people look at their thumbs with expectation as they walked away from their visit to the weeping column. He was going to turn to Weldon to ask what the guide book said about this, when he noticed that people were watching Charlotte.

She had attracted the attention from the other visitors not only because she had not joined the line, but also because of her intensely watchful stillness. She had the attitude of expectation that made those around her wonder what she was waiting for.

"Charlotte," Weldon spoke quietly to his granddaughter. "What is going on?"

She shifted closer to the column but didn't touch it. She didn't look at him but whispered, "Don't you feel it?"

Her quiet question caused Grant to startle into awareness of his surroundings. He looked around and reached out with his senses that had been honed from centuries of working with the wraiths. At first he couldn't feel anything. He was about to give up when he noticed the barest of sensations of something vaguely familiar but simultaneously foreign. He became aware that Weldon was watching him closely. Being newly recognized as a Keeper, his senses hadn't been trained and honed enough to feel it. Grant nodded to him, then bent toward him to whisper, "There is a presence. It is very faint. And it is very different."

Weldon wrinkled his brow in concern. "How different?"

Grant could only shrug his shoulders. He didn't know how to describe it and didn't have an answer to what it could mean.

Charlotte blocked out everyone around her. She had heard a faint voice calling her as soon as they had landed at the Istanbul Atatürk Airport. She had been distracted for a time because of the news they had heard about Curtis, but it had still been there, quietly calling to her. When she had gotten closer to the column, the voice had grown louder and stronger. Now that she was standing near the column, the voice was still distant but getting closer, as if it was coming to meet her at this point. It was of the same race as the wraiths, but one that had a special task that was trusted only to her.

As Charlotte stood quietly waiting, she started to hear the heartbeats of many people. She thought about her earliest vision revealed to her about the previous home of the beings they call Time Wraiths. *A pulsar, like a heartbeat in space,* she remembered as she considered the massive structure around her in the here and now. She recognized it as an ancient structure, one that had seen much of history unfold as it served humanity in its varied roles.

The voice was louder now and the speaker present. "You are making the right connections," the female voice said quietly into Charlotte's thoughts.

"Faith, hope," she mentally answered back.

"And love," the voice finished gently.

"Powerful human emotions," Charlotte mused mentally.

"Powerful states of being," the voice clarified. "Like no other in the universe."

"Ah," Charlotte's mind opened up with realization. She now had the missing piece of the puzzle. "It's not just the sound."

"No," the voice stated as the speaker started to emerge from the column. Charlotte could tell by their reactions that Grant and Weldon could see her as well.

A feminine form assembled by the column near Charlotte. She was the size of the Oracle but was made up of white mist that sparkled with tiny, brilliant flashes of energy. Her presence emanated pure peace.

"Are you the 'orb of hope'?" Charlotte asked in awe.

The entity shook her head. She gestured to the building around her. "I was placed here by the One we call the Power Above All to absorb the faith, hope, and love of humans throughout the centuries."

"Why?" Charlotte asked.

The entity sent her images throughout history and from around the world of religious paintings, crosses, and icons of Jesus. "You have been granted your means of salvation from evil." She watched Charlotte and saw her nod. "I am to equip our means of salvation from our evil."

Charlotte nodded again. She understood what the entity was saying but had growing concerns. "I am not a deity!" she countered. "I mean, if you are referring to me, I am certainly not pure or sinless!"

The entity leaned forward to stare into her eyes. "Do you believe in the Creator and His Son?"

Charlotte looked away in confusion. "Well, y-y-yes," she stammered. "I do. What has that to do with this?"

"The Creator, the Power Above All, made us all. Your belief in Him enables you to be the tool that He can use to help us. As I was the tool to gather what you needed."

"Oh," Charlotte breathed the word aloud. The revelation had her momentarily stunned.

Weldon and Grant could see the white, wispy being but couldn't hear the conversation. They watched Charlotte and the entity, wondering what was happening. All they could make out was that there was an intense conversation going on, especially with Charlotte speaking a single syllable with a quiet but serious intensity.

Grant noticed that the crowd gathering to watch them was getting larger and starting to press in toward them. He didn't want to disrupt anything, but he wanted to warn her. "Charlotte," he whispered. "We're attracting a crowd."

The being turned toward him and met his eyes. She gently broke into his thoughts. "Tell them she is having a vision. A religious experience." She smiled at him. "They will understand."

"Oh," Grant whispered back aloud. He was shocked at the clear telepathy in words instead of the wraiths' usual imagery communication. With a conscious effort, he shook off his reaction as he turned to the crowd. He was not sure that kind of explanation would work in a museum, but he felt that he had to do something before security came to escort them out.

"I am sorry," he addressed the crowd made up of all nationalities. "My girlfriend is having a vision or something. I am sure we will be moving on soon so you all can view this area."

To his surprise, they all nodded and backed away to give them space. He turned back around to watch Charlotte and face the mysterious being again. She had turned back to face Charlotte, allowing him to study her closely without her intense gaze upon him. He wondered if there was something about her that caused them to accept that explanation so readily.

The entity gave him a sidelong smile as she turned her face toward him slightly. She had picked up his thoughts. "It happens a lot here," she said simply. She turned her full attention back to Charlotte. "You have questions?"

Charlotte nodded. Her mind had processed what she had been told and was ready for more information. "Where is the 'orb of hope'? And how is it supposed to help?"

The entity studied her. "Evil's power works mainly by fear. Those that want to be evil will be, but they use fear to control others, to have power over them.

"But evil does do harm. It is not simply fear." Charlotte countered.

"It does," the entity agreed. "If it is allowed to."

"Allowed to?"

"When good is strengthened by hope, it is strong and can defeat evil."

Charlotte shut her eyes as she suddenly saw images of wars throughout the centuries. "Good eventually wins," she whispered.

The entity nodded and smiled. "Now do you see the power of hope?"

"Yes." Charlotte smiled. "Yes, I think I do."

The entity studied her even more closely and intensively for a few moments then nodded. "Yes. You are the Chosen One."

Charlotte didn't know what to do with that pronouncement. She simply smiled and waited.

The entity sighed deeply as she reached back into the column and pulled out an orb made up of golden energy. It shone brilliantly as bright white spikes shot off from different areas of the surface in a random fashion.

She reached toward Charlotte to hand it to her. Charlotte held out her hands to receive it. "It's so small." She held it between her palms as she looked at it. It was as big as a child's basketball.

"Do not be fooled about the size. It is extremely compressed," the entity warned. "I will miss having it here," she sighed.

Charlotte looked up at her "What will you do now?"

The bright entity looked around. "This is my home. With thousands of visitors a year, I can survive without affecting any one. Who knows, maybe I will continue to gather the hope of humans for another time it is needed." She shrugged her misty shoulders as she spoke. "Only the Power Above All knows."

"I see," Charlotte said, hearing the multiple heartbeats around her as she continued to look at the bright wraith. She also worried deep down if she could accomplish what she needed to do.

"Yes, I will come if you need help," the white, misty being said quietly.

"What is your name?" Charlotte asked respectfully.

"Pandora," she answered as she reached out with a long, slender, luminous arm to tap the orb on the top with delicate and lengthy fingers.

"Pandora of myth? The one that let evil out into the world?" Charlotte asked as she watched the orb dissolve and absorb into her body.

Pandora smiled as she shook her head, causing the white, wispy tendrils of hair to float about her head and face. "No. I am the Pandora that will let Hope into the world."

"But the hope depicted in the myth has been described as small and frail," Charlotte said as she dropped her empty hands to her sides. She was surprised that she could continue to think as she felt the power from the orb race through her being and fill her with unexpected strength.

"Not anymore," Pandora replied as she disappeared into the column.

Charlotte shivered. She wasn't sure if it was because of the effects of the orb dissolving into her body or from what had been revealed to her.

Grant immediately put his coat around her and held her when he saw her shivering. "Let's go," he whispered to Weldon.

"It appears the vision was very intense," Weldon announced to the ever larger crowd.

A voice came from the mass of people crowding the surrounding area. "Can it be revealed to us?"

Weldon looked at Grant. Grant shook his head as he held Charlotte, who was limp in his arms.

"Yes," another called out. "With everything happening in the world, we need hope."

At the word 'hope,' Charlotte stood up and shook off Grant and his coat. "Yes! Hope!" she announced to the crowd, her voice loud and clear to all in the building. "There is hope. No matter what happens, look to Hope, Faith, and Love," she said clearly to all. "They are the strongest forces in this universe."

With those words, her spurt of energy was spent. Grant caught her as she sagged to the floor. Wrapping his coat around her again, he picked her up in his arms. With Weldon clearing a path, they made their way out of the building and into the hired car where their driver waited.

CHAPTER TWENTY-SEVEN

After leaving the Hagia Sophia, they had the driver take them back to their hotel. They rode in silence as Grant and Weldon worried about Charlotte. She looked extremely drained. Although she was very pale, she seemed to emit a faint, golden glow.

Grant wasn't sure what to think about what he had witnessed. He wasn't sure what Weldon thought, as they had their full attention on Charlotte and her condition. After they had made sure she was settled in her bedroom and tucked comfortably in her bed, they softly closed the door and sat on the couch in the suite's common area.

They didn't speak for a long while as they pondered their own perspectives of their experiences. Weldon worried about his granddaughter while Grant was in shock about meeting yet another of the wraith race that was different but yet mysteriously the same. Eventually, he shook off the mental cobwebs and ran his fingers through his hair. Weldon saw that he was snapping out of his stupor. "So, what do you think?" he asked.

Grant met his eyes, then looked away toward the closed bedroom door. "I think that whatever is coming up, she should be well equipped."

Weldon nodded, then frowned. "That may be, but what is coming up, when, and where?"

Grant shook his head. He sighed as he sat back deeper into the couch. "I'm hoping she'll have more information once she's rested."

They fell back into a quiet contemplation as the silence grew heavier around them. They were so deep in their own thoughts that they didn't think about doing anything else and wound up falling asleep.

They were still asleep when Charlotte woke up before dawn the next morning. She discovered them sprawled out on opposite ends of the couch, heads thrown back and snoring. She imagined they were having a contest to see who could snore the loudest. Smiling, she shook her head as she watched them.

Looking around the room, she started to bite her lower lip as she contemplated what she was going to do. She decided to make a choice for the moment, since the future was still not certain. It was a small thing, but she decided to sit in one of the chairs facing toward the couch. She needed to be near those she trusted the most in all the world. After she sat down, Becker came to hover near her.

Charlotte looked up at her smoky face. "So what do you think?"

Becker shrugged her shoulders.

Charlotte studied her closely. "Any chance I'll hear your voice again?"

Becker smiled mysteriously but didn't offer anything else.

Charlotte glanced at her men, still having their snoring contest, then leaned back into the overstuffed armchair. Resting her head on top of the cushion of the chair back, she rubbed her forehead. After she settled her hands in her lap, she opened her eyes to stare at the ceiling. "I have no idea what's supposed to happen next." She shifted her head enough to look at Becker. Still no reaction or response from the floating wraith. She resumed her former contemplation of the ceiling. "Do you have any idea what's going to happen and when?"

Becker moved to float over her, positioning herself face to face with Charlotte. She slowly shook her head as she met her eyes.

Charlotte smiled at her wearily. "Okay. I guess I have to be patient and wait."

Becker nodded at her rapidly in hearty agreement. After she had moved out of sight, Charlotte continued to look at the ceiling until she fell back asleep.

When Grant woke up, his first waking thought was silently cursing the crick in his neck. As he rubbed the pain out of his neck while he lifted his head, his second thought superseded the first, for he saw Charlotte curled up in a chair near him. He watched her for a while as he admired her relaxed face and watched her slow, deep breathing. When he heard snoring coming from the other end of the couch, he stiffly turned to see Weldon sleeping soundly with head back and arms flung out to his sides. As he studied each one of them in turn, he thought of how much things had changed in the short time since he had first seen these two sleeping in the same room. Less than a year ago, Charlotte had also been curled up in a chair but Weldon had been on his death bed.

Suddenly a jaw-popping yawn overcame him. Once he was able to close his mouth, he rubbed his face, noting the prickly stubble, and ran his fingers through his tousled, curly hair. Standing up, he stretched his arms above his head as he arched his back. As every joint popped and complained of being aggravated, he frowned as he thought of how long he had been away from his clockworks room. He hoped he would be able to get back home soon and have time to rejuvenate.

He glanced at the sleeping pair to make sure his movements didn't disturb them. As they continued to sleep soundly, he smiled and nodded to himself. Carefully, he made his way to the balcony doors and eased them open to step outside.

From the eastwardly facing balcony, he watched the sun rise over the city of Istanbul. From this vantage point, he could see the Hagia Sophia. As he watched the daylight becoming brighter and revealing more detail in and around the ancient city, he wondered what was next.

Grant felt more than saw the wraith sidle up next to him. He turned his head to see who it was but didn't recognize him. When he tried to communicate with the shadowy being, he couldn't understand the fast flow of visual images. He was about to call Becker, when she showed up with Grant, the wraith.

He watched as the shadowy being communicated a message to the other two. Once the message was delivered, the wraith flew off, leaving Becker and Grant, the wraith, to confer amongst themselves. As he watched them, he began to wonder what was going on. To him, their gestures and expressions seemed to convey that something serious was happening. When Grant, the wraith, flew off, it was obvious that he was sent on a mission.

Grant was about to ask Becker for information when she flowed through the balcony doors and turned to beckon him within. Opening the glass doors, he stepped back indoors and closed them behind him carefully. Once he was inside, she gestured to the sleeping pair. She wanted him to wake them up.

Apparently this is for all of us to hear, Grant thought as he gently jostled Charlotte and her grandfather awake. Once they were alert and before they could ask questions, he pointed to Becker, who was floating in the middle of the room, waiting.

When she knew she had their full attention, Becker showed them the images she had formed from her communication with the wraith messenger. She had made sure to relay the message in the visual form that she knew these Keepers could understand.

When they saw the face of one of the European Keepers, Weldon piped up, "That's the Keeper who is watching the tower clock mechanism from the warehouse."

The next image was the tower clock and the Sentinel that resided in it talking to the wraith messenger. She stopped to make sure they were aware of where the message was coming from. They nodded at her that they understood who sent the message she was about to share.

Next she showed them a mental image of a ring of large standing stones. "Stonehenge?" they all asked in unison. Becker nodded to confirm, then waited.

Charlotte was biting her lower lip as she thought. Grant and Weldon glanced at each other. They both felt they knew what the image meant, but they let Charlotte ask the question. "Is that where it will happen?" she asked after several quiet minutes. Becker nodded slowly as she met her eyes.

"Do we know when?" Weldon, ever practical about details, asked quietly. Becker shook her head, then made a gesture with her hands.

"Oh," Charlotte responded in understanding. Weldon and Grant looked from Becker to her in confusion. She noted their reaction. "That's a sign meaning…well…" she stumbled as she thought through possible definitions, trying to find the best one. She nodded to herself as she found one that was most appropriate. "We would say 'in their court.'"

"Meaning it's up to the opposition?" Grant asked to clarify. Both Charlotte and Becker nodded to confirm.

"So we wait?" Weldon asked clearly uncomfortable with what he heard.

"We wait," Grant stated gruffly. Worry and frustration roughened his voice. He sat back down on the couch as he crossed his arms over his chest. He was glad they had some sort of news, but the waiting and watching was wearing on him. He wanted whatever was going to happen to be over and done with.

Charlotte leaned over to place a hand on his knee. In response, he met her eyes. She smiled slightly and nodded that she understood his feelings and was feeling the same. "It will be soon," she whispered. "I am almost sure of that." He smiled at her and tried to make an effort to relax.

On the other end of the couch, Weldon had pulled out his phone. "I would say we need to head back to England." He looked up at both of them when no comment was made. "Don't you think? So we can be ready when it is time?"

Grant and Charlotte looked at each other, then at Becker. Grant turned to Weldon to speak for them. "Might as well," he said with a shrug.

As Weldon made arrangements, Grant took the opportunity to step back out on the balcony. He looked over a city that was now awake and bustling. *I hope I can come back someday to explore this city further,* he thought as he leaned against the railing.

Charlotte slipped out of the room to stand next to him. She glanced at him looking out over the city and leaned against the railing. After a few minutes, she sighed. "I hope to come back," she said quietly. "I would like to see more of this city and the Hagia Sophia."

Grant glanced over at her and smiled. "I was thinking the same thing," he said quietly.

CHAPTER TWENTY-EIGHT

This was their battlefield. The chosen ones for good and for evil had arrived at the ancient ring of standing stones. Charlotte had taken the rental car, leaving Grant and her grandfather sleeping in the hotel room they had gotten a few days earlier in Salisbury, England. The summons in the wee hours of the night had been so urgent and abruptly demanding that her only thoughts were to get to Stonehenge as soon as possible.

As she parked the car as close as she could to the monument, she peered through the dark that was lit only by starlight. She thought of the details of the area from when they had visited a few days earlier, right after they had arrived back in England. She hadn't been aware until then that security measures had been put into place a few years before because of vandalism. She had taken special note of the chain link fence around the entire area since it was her biggest boundary. The only remaining one after that was a rope that kept visitors on the cement walkway that went around the standing stones. She still wondered if there would be guards that watched the area at night.

She got out of the car and looked around. She didn't see any hints of security but remained alert in case she sensed any movement as she approached the fence. With no one to interrupt her, she went to work on the chain link. Bending down, she untwisted the bottom link then stretched up try to undo the top link. The fence was high enough that she had to partially climb it to reach the top link. With those undone, she was able to unweave one of the wires. When it was removed without damaging the fence, she was able to pull a section apart to allow her to walk through. Laying the wire aside so that the fence could be pieced back together, she continued toward the standing stones.

After she crossed over the cement path and over the rope, she started to sense the presence of the great evil. She stopped to ascertain the focal point. Soon she was able to pinpoint it at the opposite side of the large standing stones from her.

She took a deep breath and started walking again. The ancient stones blocked her view of whoever the evil entity was using as its host. She prayed it was not her brother, but since he had dropped out of sight with no word about where he was or what he was doing, they feared it would be him. As she thought of her brother, she remembered her hot anger at him when she sought help from Grant months ago. Now all she could feel was pity for her twisted sibling.

Her mind was drawn away from thoughts of Curtis as she realized that she sensed a great power coming from the area. It was not the evil entity. It was something she had never experienced before. She noticed that it intensified as she drew nearer to the Sarsen stones. As the upright blocks of bluestone loomed over her as she got closer, she marveled how a few of them still held their lintels high above the ground even after centuries of time. She stopped to stand under one of the lintels to peer across the smaller stones within the heart of Stonehenge as she contemplated the presence she sensed.

She was distracted from trying to figure out if the power present was residual or sentient when she saw a movement. The starlight was enough that she could see a figure opposite her, also standing between two of the great standing stones. Her heart sank when she recognized the shape and stance and knew that it was her brother. Even the power that enveloped the area could not dampen the sense of the evil entity that seethed and oozed from him.

"You can decline to be part of this!" she shouted to him. "You can demand it to release you! I can show you how!"

"I don't want it to!" her brother growled harshly back at her. "I welcome it!!"

"Why?" she shouted back. She was truly mystified by his response.

"The power!" he exclaimed as he lifted his arms over his head. "I am powerful! I am somebody that cannot be ignored!"

Charlotte could see the green-black energy bolts glow dully in the dark as they shot back and forth between his arms. She shook her head sadly. "It is a deception," she shouted back. "That power will devour you when it is done using you."

"No! It won't!" he screeched, sounding increasingly demented. The evil energy intensified as the bolts became larger and more frequent. "I, only I, am in control!!"

"That is the lie! That is the deception!" she shouted back. She truly wanted him to understand. She slowly moved closer to him as she started to carefully weave around the smaller stones.

He noticed her moving as he brought down his arms. "You stay there!" he shouted as he pointed at her. The sneer that twisted his face was highlighted in the eerie glow of the dull green energy from his outstretched arm. "Miss Goody Two Shoes, Miss Perfect... I will destroy you! As I have wanted to do all my life!"

Charlotte shook her head. The words tried to enter her mind and heart to hurt her. She brushed them aside. She knew bigger things were at risk, and she didn't want the distraction of sibling conflicts to get in the way. "Not likely," she muttered to herself.

"What?!" Curtis shouted. "What are you saying?!" He stomped toward her, waving his fists. Green-black bolts of power flared from his knuckles.

Charlotte sensed movement behind her. She turned around, expecting it to be Grant and her grandfather. No, it wasn't them. She did see that they had finally caught up with her but were still getting out of a car that was parked on the plains outside Stonehenge. Instead, she saw Becker and a huge army of wraiths behind her. She turned to look behind Curtis in the gradually lightening horizon. She nodded to herself as she saw another army of wraiths behind him. She knew those were all the available bad boys of the alien beings. She was glad the Sentinels still held hundreds of their kind to weaken their ranks.

After her assessment of the situation, she calmly looked at Curtis. "This is between you and me," she announced as he grew closer while he weaved through the stones from his direction.

"Me and my evil friend," he sneered back. "Against you, and only you!" he chuckled evilly. "You have no one to stand with you!!'

"Oh," she smiled back peacefully. "I am not alone." As she had practiced over the days leading to this moment, she telepathically opened the orb that was deep within her. Even through the slightest slit of an opening, she felt hope fill and strengthen her as it had when she first absorbed it. By the time she had opened it up completely, she blazed with a white light that emitted the energy of hope in bright silver waves that pulsed outward from her.

Curtis stopped suddenly to stare at her. "What?" He looked confused as the evil miasma started to ooze out of him. "What is that?"

The power that emanated from her caused her soft voice to sound clear and loud, like true tones from a silver bell, to every being in the area. "It is the hope of mankind throughout the centuries. The hope that not only survived, but thrived, through all the world's events, no matter how terrible." The bright power completely engulfed her as it gently lifted her off the ground to levitate her to the level of the top of the Sarsen stones. She shone as brightly as the sun, illuminating the area inside and outside Stonehenge as the predawn blush of sunrise faded from the senses with her power.

* * * * * * *

Grant and Weldon had found the downed section of chain link fence. They had gotten as far as the ring of standing stones before they stopped to watch the unfolding scene. Grant shaded his eyes as he marveled how Charlotte looked much like a wingless angel. He wanted to step in and help but didn't know how he could be of much use in the face of the magnitude of the power he was seeing displayed in front of them. Feeling useless, he crossed his arms over his chest and stood in the background.

Weldon felt Grant shift and turned to study him. He noted the set of the other man's jaw, the hard stare and the tense stance. "We may still be needed in this," he whispered to the taller man. He wanted to gently remind him that he wasn't alone in having to stay in the background of the unfolding events.

Grant slightly turned his head to give him a half-smile and nodded at him that he had heard. But as he faced forward again, his mouth set in a firm line as his eyes hardened into protective fierceness. He did not like the fact that he was helpless on the sidelines when he should be protecting her. He knew that it was a silly thought in the light of the massive power she wielded, but he still felt that he should protect her nonetheless. Suddenly, he felt powerful presences behind him.

Both Grant and Weldon turned to see Pandora and the Oracle gliding in to take their positions behind them. Both their mouths dropped open as the mighty wraiths hovered as they also waited.

"We, too, are of no use right now," Pandora told them. "This must be fought between the Chosen Ones of good and evil. Our time for action will come in its own time."

Grant nodded at them as he turned back to watch. He caught Weldon's eye and gave him a more genuine smile. He felt a bit better.

* * * * * * *

The evil entity pulled back into Curtis. Charlotte wasn't sure whether it was hiding or reinforcing itself. She floated nearer to her brother. She addressed the evil entity directly. "If you leave us in peace, we will not follow." She delivered the chance for it to get away from the awesome power she wielded. "If you don't, you will be destroyed."

She saw the wraiths behind Curtis look at each other uncertainly. She noticed their expression shift to despair as if they were caged, then desperation because they had no choice but to support their evil oppressor.

She tried to contact Becker to warn her before her forces leapt into action that it was going to be a fight to the death.

The enemy had nothing to lose. But there wasn't enough time. The opposing forces were already on the move toward each other. She could see they would clash over the altar stone in the middle of Stonehenge.

When both wraith armies engaged, the sudden, violent clash sounded like a lightening crack to all the Keepers in the area. The roiling cloud of battling wraiths obscured the visibility between the siblings. The shrieks and cries of battle interfered with Charlotte's thoughts and perceptions. That was the only way she could've been surprised by what happened next.

Curtis suddenly dove through the black clouds and tackled her. He had leapt off the altar stone to grab her by her feet and slam her to the ground. Once Charlotte impacted the hard ground between the smaller stones, she could not only feel the physical weight of Curtis but also the smothering weight of the fear and despair the evil miasma emanated.

She mentally reached out to the ambient power in the area to see if it would be a help or a hindrance to her. When she realized that it would remain neutral, she understood why this location had been chosen. With its presence, the battle would be contained to prevent harm to the world.

Curtis mercilessly held her down as he dug his knees into her belly and roughly ground her shoulders against the ground with his hands. His eyes glowed a menacing green while he smiled manically as he saw that she clawed at the hard soil underneath her. He cackled gleefully as he saw that the entity's sensation of fear, like a huge boa, wrapped itself around her and squeezed. Soon she was gasping painfully for breath as she physically could not pull enough air into her lungs and as she felt her inner self being cruelly and relentlessly crushed.

The radiance of hope from the orb seemed to dim, then disappear. She scrambled around within herself looking for the weapons of love and hope that she and Grant had successfully used against the entity before. But in the pressure cooker of an evil that had been further enhanced by the willing bonding of a human, they were nowhere to be found. She felt absolutely alone and completely powerless. She felt achingly empty and began to wilt into hopelessness.

* * * * * * *

Grant had run toward her through the obstacle course of stones when he saw Curtis tackle her and the bright light disappear. As he got closer to the altar stone, he hit a wall of evil as he tried to get to her. He struggled against the barrier as he watched for Charlotte to tap the power he had seen in her before. When time seemed to stop as she lay limp under the storm cloud of battling wraiths, he feared the worst. Curtis had moved away from her and was hidden from him. But he still felt the evil buffet him from all sides and wondered if he would be physically attacked by his love's crazed sibling.

He soon forgot about Curtis when he realized that the evil entity was stronger than when it tried to attack Charlotte and him before. Through the physical and mental agony he fought to endure, he realized that the bonding with Curtis empowered the entity even further. This was not a case of possession, it was a willing symbiosis.

As the evil presence worked to disable him with fear and hopelessness, Grant scrambled to find the link that had been forged between him and Charlotte. It was tenuous, but he mentally grasped it with all he had and willed his strength to her.

* * * * * * *

Suddenly, when all looked to be lost, she sensed the lifeline that Grant had thrown her. It was as fragile as an eggshell, but it caused her to rouse from her stupor so she could cast around again for anything to use to fight back. With a renewed sense of stubborn survival, she discovered, still deep within herself, a bright spark barely the size of a dust mote. She had never been left alone! She had simply lost sight of it. The orb of hope had shrunk as the pressure of the evil pounded at her from every side while it waited for her to act. It was not weakened nor defeated but it needed her to fully believe in its power, even in the face of overwhelming forces, and to wield it.

From that point, she refused to allow the fear and despair to take her over completely. As she mentally touched the spark again, this time fully believing in its existence and in its undefeatable power, it instantly responded by expanding like an exploding sun. As the even more intense white light burst forth from her, it sheared through the battling wraiths. The waves of power empowered the good and weakened the bad. Soon the battle of wraiths was over. But the battle between evil and hope was not complete.

The sudden explosion of power threw Grant back to the ring of the giant standing stones. The impact against one of them knocked him out. After several minutes, he awoke to find Weldon standing over him and the sounds of hand to hand combat coming from the area of the altar stone.

The possessed Curtis had recoiled from the light and power but did not run. Once the evil entity regrouped within its human host, it attacked Charlotte with a shriek that was inhuman and chilled Grant and Weldon to the bone. The onslaught was vicious as Curtis hit and kicked his sister. Charlotte grimly defended herself without giving any ground. This time she had been ready for him as she stood ready to take him on.

At first, they seemed evenly matched. But when the evil reached out to grab for her again, the power of hope grabbed it and yanked it completely out of Curtis. Once the evil entity was free of the human, the orb of hope reassembled outside of Charlotte.

The orb quickly surrounded and entrapped the green-black cloud with bright, shimmering light. Once the evil was contained, it squeezed and condensed itself into the size of the orb as Charlotte had first seen it. As she watched, the orb squeezed down smaller and smaller until it was a bright spot the size of a small coin. It shone so brilliantly, she had to shield her eyes with a hand. Suddenly, it squeezed down one last time with a brilliant flash that blinded everyone for a moment. Once their vision cleared, they saw a golden mist where the orb had hovered. Slowly, the bright mist dissipated in the air as it scattered in all directions. Hope had destroyed the evil, leaving no trace.

Charlotte sat on the ground suddenly. She was completely and utterly spent. After days of anticipating this event, she was glad it was over but felt empty.

No, she thought as she sensed a residue of the orb and the power of hope remain deeply embedded in her being. *There is still hope. There is always hope.* She smiled to herself.

She looked up at her brother, who still stood nearby but looked confused and lost. As she slowly stood and brushed herself off, she found that she was starting to hurt in various places. She looked at her hands bloodied by the fight and broken finger nails. She rubbed her chest, belly, legs, and arms, feeling sore spots that she knew would be bruises by the next day.

When she heard a moan, her attention focused on her brother. "Curtis?" she asked gently as she slowly approached him. "Curtis? Are you okay?" She noticed he had a bloody nose, bruised knuckles, and the beginnings of a black eye.

Curtis looked at her with perplexed but vacant eyes. "What happened? Where am I?" He didn't seem to realize that he was injured.

"You are okay," she answered, grimacing in pain as she put an arm around his shoulders. She breathed a quick prayer of thanks when she sensed nothing left of the evil entity. She doubted that all of his badness had been stripped away but was glad it was no longer enhanced. "We will take care of you."

"Yes, we will," said a voice nearby. Charlotte looked around to see Grant and Weldon closing in on them quickly. "I have called for help," Weldon was saying as he hugged Charlotte, then stopped when he felt her wince in pain. He quickly looked her over to assess her injuries. When he was sure that there was nothing serious, he took Curtis from her arm and looked him over.

Grant took advantage of her being free of her family and investigated her wounds thoroughly. As he gently probed the wounds on her face and felt for anything broken, he gently asked her if she was in severe pain. She shook her head, then put a hand to her neck as the bruised muscles burned in pain. "Do you need to go to the hospital?" he asked in concern.

"No," she said firmly. When he had turned his head slightly, she stopped him. She reached up and felt blood in his hair. When she probed further, he winced in pain as she found a large goose egg developing. "I think you need to go. What happened?"

He gently removed her hand and held it in his. "I had a close encounter with an ancient stone," he said as he tried to smile through the dull headache that was developing.

"I'm sorry," she murmured as she looked in his face. "Was it because of the battle?"

He gave her a lopsided grin and shrugged. "I guess you could say that." He gently drew her into his arms, trying to be careful with all her injuries. He just wanted to hold her for a moment, glad that she was okay and that the battle was over.

After a while, she tapped his shoulder. "I do need to breathe," she said quietly. She smiled at him as he loosened his hold.

"Sorry," he whispered as he backed away slightly. "I am glad you are okay."

She studied his face, then smiled as she carefully stroked his whiskered cheek and chin. "You forgot to shave."

He rubbed his face. "I forgot. You disappeared this morning." His expression held a poorly veiled accusation.

She hung her head. "I'm sorry. I had to move quickly. It was time."

"We were ready to go at a drop of a hat," Grant chided her.

Charlotte stared into his eyes and saw deep emotions of hurt and betrayal. She could also see that he was searching her eyes for something. Something he didn't see as looked away and started to turn to leave.

"Look, Charlotte," he was beginning to say, "I know you don't feel for me as ..." he was stopped abruptly as she grabbed handfuls of his shirt despite painful hands, jerked him toward her, ignoring aching muscles, and kissed him passionately despite a split, sore lip. When she let him go, he was stunned and unable to speak. She hoped she hadn't aggravated a possible concussion

"I love you, too," she said quietly as she looked deeply into his eyes. She was making sure he was focusing on her and that his pupils were equal. "I have ever since I met you. It just took me this long to admit it to you and myself." She couldn't judge his expression as he swept her into a giant hug that started off tight, but quickly loosened when he felt her involuntarily wince.

When they separated again, they looked around to see that a widely grinning Weldon waited for them nearby. They also saw that Curtis was being led away by a group of uniformed people. Weldon had flown in a team from the mental hospital in case Curtis showed up in the area. Weldon was about to say something when he stopped as he stared at something that was behind them in the confines of the heart of Stonehenge.

When Charlotte and Grant saw Weldon's expression, they turned to look over their shoulders. What they saw made them forget their injuries and turn fully toward the ancient site to stand and watch. Pandora and the Oracle were talking with the multitudes of wraiths from both armies that were still in the area.

"What are they talking about?" Grant asked Charlotte without taking his eyes from the scene.

"I don't know." She shook her head slightly as she tried to make out the words. "It's another language. I believe it is their native tongue."

"How can you not understand it?" Grant was mystified. "The new arrivals had talked with you."

"Remember, I said they had communicated with me in a fashion. They still had to use a type of imaging for communication. They reached out only to me for some reason."

Soon they saw the captive wraiths being pulled toward Pandora. It was obvious to the onlookers that she asked each of them a question. If they nodded, she touched them and they were free to go. If they shook their heads, she didn't and they continued to be held captive.

"I think those that want to be cleared of the evil taint are," Charlotte observed.

"I guess we still need to fix our vaults," Grant muttered as he noted several wraiths refuse her touch.

"Yes," Charlotte agreed as she also monitored the process.

When all the captive wraiths had been presented to Pandora and the remaining ones dispersed, Charlotte limped between the large standing stones to approach Pandora and the Oracle.

They looked her over, taking note of her injuries. "We are sorry for your physical discomfort," they both said quietly.

Charlotte shook her head carefully. "It is not bad," she said dismissively. She wanted to know more details and knew they would be the ones to ask.

"She has questions," the Oracle stated.

"Of course," Pandora smiled. "Curiosity. Another human strength."

"Is the evil entity gone for good?" Charlotte asked.

"That evil born out of our people's misdeeds has been destroyed. That particular entity won't be able to wreak destruction anymore."

"Does that mean there is no evil amongst your people anymore?"

"Oh, there are those who like to be bad, for there is a wrongness that threads through this creation." Pandora said. "Those that follow that path are an irritant but unable to cause mass destruction." She glanced over at the Oracle, and they exchanged a knowing look. Pandora turned back to meet Charlotte's eyes. "However, another evil entity can be brought forth again. It was the actions of Society that created the one that has been finally dealt with. We need to safeguard our ways so that it will be less likely to happen again."

"For future world events, look to your own hand," the Oracle said. "For humanity's steps in destiny and solution, look to that the Creator of all things gave to mankind."

Charlotte was momentarily confused by the Oracle's words. She quickly filed them away in her memory, figuring that someday it would be clarified. "What will your people do now?" Charlotte asked quietly. She worried about the answer.

"What do your people want us to do?" Pandora asked.

"The ones who know about you would like for you to stay, if you can," Charlotte answered, feeling she was speaking for all the Keepers.

The white, misty entity nodded thoughtfully. "Since there is more known about us, perhaps we can be of more service to mankind."

"Yes," Charlotte nodded back, excitement acting like a temporary natural pain killer. "I can imagine that a coalition could be advantageous." She was relieved to know that they wouldn't be leaving. She looked down as she tried to think of more questions while they were both with her. But the two entities were finished.

"Chosen One," the Oracle said, getting Charlotte's attention. "You know where to find me."

"And," Pandora said as she smiled, "you know where I am."

Charlotte smiled and honored each one with a slight, stiff bow. Both entities bowed to her, then flowed swiftly out of sight, their white, misty forms disappearing into the full light of the newly risen sun.

Charlotte walked back to where Grant and Weldon waited outside the ring of standing stones. "Let's go home," she said to them as she limped past them toward their parked cars.

Grant and Weldon looked at each other, then back at her. "Really? We can go home?" they asked at the same time.

Charlotte didn't even look back as she shook her head and signaled to them with a careful wave of an aching arm to follow her.

Once everyone was past the gap in the fence, she stopped and picked up the wire. She was going to weave it back in to repair the chain link. Grant stopped to stand by her and silently took it from her. As he pulled the section of fence together with her and Weldon's help, he asked, "How did you know to do this?"

As she watched him carefully weave the wire back into place, she replied, "I would follow the ranch hands around on my parent's land. I learned how to fix barb wire fences as well as chain link." She glanced at her grandfather to see his reaction. He smiled widely as he shook his head slightly. "Came in handy!"

"That it did," Grant responded as he finished the job. "Did you ever see security?" he said as he looked around.

"No," she shook her head. "I figure if there was any, I bet Becker made sure they were distracted."

Grant looked around, then back at the fence, which looked as if it had never been touched. "That is good. No one will ever know what happened here."

Charlotte looked down at her bleeding hands and felt her split lip. She looked up at the blood on Grant's head and thought of Curtis' injuries. Glancing over at the ancient site, she muttered, "As long as they don't have a forensics team come out here."

Weldon heard her as he looked sharply back at Stonehenge. "Do you think they will have cause to?"

Grant considered what she said as he saw the mental hospital team drive away, starting their journey back home. "I don't think anyone will have any reason to report this." He looked at Weldon, "Didn't you have the mental health people sign a nondisclosure agreement?"

Weldon smiled and nodded. "I did. Had no idea what they would witness while they were here."

Charlotte smiled as they started to walk slowly toward their car. "So the only ones to know are we, the wraiths, and, eventually, their Keepers," she said, knowing that the wraiths would pass the word around to their human companions.

CHAPTER TWENTY-NINE

After weeks of being away, Grant stood in front of his clock shop. He was finally home. Overhead, the sun was shining brightly from a clear sky but was not noticed by him as he pondered what he saw. He was surprised that his shop was open as customers went in and out of the front door.

Curious and concerned, he walked through the glass doors to see what was going on. He was surprised to find John and Winston running the place. "Well, hello!" He smiled slightly as he clasped both of their hands to shake them in turn as he greeted them. "What happened here?"

"We got bored," John muttered. "He had nothing to do. I had nothing to do. He had your key to feed Gustav."

Grant looked confused. "I had a pet sitter watching him," he said as he looked around for his large tabby cat.

John sat back on the stool behind the counter to put his booted feet up on the wood surface. "Yeah, well, you were gone so long, and she needed to go somewhere." He also looked around. "He was just here. I think he went upstairs. He hasn't been happy with you gone."

Winston wrung his hands. He had been worried that their forward actions would be taken badly when Grant got back. He had been persuaded by John that this was the right thing. "You had left my number with her for emergencies," he said meekly.

Grant nodded and smiled. "So while you were taking care of Gustav, why not open the shop?"

John dropped his feet to the floor to reach over the counter. He pulled Grant closer to him to whisper, "I told everyone you were on vacation. A long-deserved vacation. And that you would do repairs when you got back. We've just been doing sales."

"Was that okay?" Winston still wasn't sure, even though Grant was smiling.

"Yes, Winston," he clapped the butler on the shoulder, "it is quite all right! Thank you!" Grant said warmly, truly appreciating their efforts. "Quite a surprise!" He looked at John. "What about your shop?"

John smiled. "My assistant can handle it. Plus my wraiths will let me know if there is a problem."

John stood up and signaled Winston to take over watching the shop while he pulled Grant into the back room. "You're going to have to tell me everything, but right now, most of the wraiths got here days ago! They wouldn't tell me why you were delayed!"

Grant smiled. "I told them not to. I wanted to tell you in person."

"Tell me what?" John looked suspicious. "Hey," he poked his head through the curtain to look back into the showroom. "Where's Charlotte?"

"She'll be here," Grant said with a smile. "She's bringing the rest of her stuff over from her grandfather's estate..."

"She's moving in?" John interrupted him in shocked surprised. "You mean I don't have a chance?"

"Afraid not." Grant smiled more widely. "While we were in Europe, we got married." John's face immediately fell. Grant saw his deep disappointment. "Hey, man, didn't know you felt that way about her."

"Oh, dude," John looked at the floor. "I mean, I like her." He looked up to frown at Grant. "But you didn't invite me to the wedding!"

Grant was immediately relieved. "Hey, it was a very small affair. However, we're having a service and reception here for family and the American Keepers." He clapped him on the back. "You're definitely invited to that!"

John grinned brightly and gave Grant a quick hug. "Awesome, dude!

* * * * * * *

Charlotte and Weldon stood in front of a group of clocks grouped in the middle of the ballroom and walled off by a thick ring of silver cubes. Becker had told her that when John had found out about the situation, he came down to help secure the royals better. He had moved the clocks they had been imprisoned in so that they were in one place so they would be easier for the wraiths to guard. He also placed all the cubes he could find around them, figuring the more the better.

She had heard from Becker about the royal family and their taint from the evil. Becker had also implied to Charlotte that it was unlikely the royals would agree to the new normal of their race. They had been in power for centuries before they had to flee their homes. Now that they were in their new home, they had expected to pick up where they had left off.

She sighed deeply, then turned away. She wondered if Pandora could help them. She also wondered if the grey-silver wall of cubes that had been built would hold them.

She was also worried what would happen if they escaped. Becker had implied that the royals were more powerful than a typical wraith.

She turned to leave, then glanced over her shoulder. She wondered if they were truly confined or waiting to get stronger before they made their move.

Weldon watched his granddaughter, then looked at the clocks. "Will I need to keep them here? I was hoping to use the ballroom for the reception."

Charlotte bit her lower lip as she thought. "They could probably be moved. It would be better to split them up and have them in a vault. That would be more secure."

"Have they figured out what Carlos did to the vaults?" Weldon asked.

"I don't think so," she answered thoughtfully. She was distracted from those thoughts when she saw Winston entering the room. "Hello, Winston." Charlotte hugged the butler. "Good to see you!"

"And I, you, mistress!" Winston grinned and blushed with emotion from the attention she bestowed on him. "I just came from the clock shop! I overheard Grant talking with John. Congratulations, mistress!" His grin stretched even further in pure delight. Then he sobered as he gazed at her with a look of watchful expectation.

"Winston," Charlotte held both of his hands as she faced him. "I would be honored if you would arrange the festivities."

Sheer joy spread across his lean features. "I... mistress... I would be pleased and honored!" He let go of her hands and happily stood ramrod straight and bowed formally and deeply from the waist. "I will commence immediately," he announced, then smartly spun on his heels. Charlotte and Weldon glanced at each other as they both tried to suppress a laugh as they saw their manservant speed away with a telltale skip in the step of his long legs.

Weldon moved closer to his granddaughter to whisper, "You have made him very happy!"

"I am glad," she smiled brightly. Then a shadow fell over it briefly as she glanced back at the clocks. The presences she sensed made her uneasy.

EPILOGUE

Weeks later, John tracked Grant down as he was taking a break in the back room of his shop. "Some other news, dude," he started. "The Keepers from this side of the pond figured out what happened to the vaults."

"Really?" Grant was surprised and pleased. "What happened?" He sat back in the chair as he put his coffee cup down.

"When you found that Carlos Lopez was the evil Keeper, someone over here recognized he was part of the crew that would install, maintain, and upgrade the vaults." John continued as he sat down in a chair opposite from Grant.

Grant nodded that he followed. He was anxious to have the last piece of this puzzle in place.

"A group of Keepers went to one of their vaults, dug it up, and disassembled the whole thing. They found that the link between the rewind mechanism and the springs was designed to blow with a very specific signal. The resulting explosion damaged the springs, instantly causing the clockworks to stop and opening the vaults."

Grant's face fell in shock. He stood up and started to pace while running his fingers through his hair. "When was the last upgrade? A hundred years ago?" he muttered angrily as he threw out numbers without thinking. "He planned all this that far in advance?"

At first, John mutely nodded. Grant's reaction mirrored his own when he had heard the news. After a few moments, he said quietly, "They told me they thought the alterations were installed several decades ago with the last round of upgrades. That was the last time everyone's vaults had been worked on."

Grant stopped pacing. He dropped his hands and clenched them at his sides. "This doesn't make sense," he muttered darkly. He started pacing again. "I thought all this had been brought about by the great evil coming on earth. But that can't be the case." He looked at John, his eyes bleak with deep concern. "Was it just a coincidence?" He stopped again. "How did Carlos get involved with the evil entity?" He met John's eyes as he sought more information.

The other Keeper looked at him thoughtfully. "I think I can answer that." He stood up to stand closer to Grant so he could talk quietly with him. "When Winston collected his pocket watches, he noticed that he was missing one."

"Really?"

John nodded. "Yes, a 1680 single-handed French Oignon pocket watch. Not only was it big but it was also a beauty." He pulled out his phone to show Grant a picture of one on Ebay. "When we ruled out that it was misplaced somewhere, we figured it was stolen."

Grant rubbed his chin as he thought. "Becker told me that the royals had been tainted because one of them was possessed."

"Once we got more pieces to this puzzle, that's what we thought." John looked around, then back at Grant. "Somehow, Carlos had stolen that pocket watch and got unlucky in what it carried."

"Or it influenced him to pick up that particular pocket watch," Grant thought out loud. "Evil can be persuasive, and he was already bent in that direction."

"True," John agreed.

Grant suddenly snapped his fingers. "That's how Curtis knew we were at the mansion."

"When you tossed him out?" John grinned.

"Yeah." He hit his palm with his fist. "That's how he knew."

"It fits." John nodded.

"Okay," Grant muttered to himself. "Yes, it all seems to make sense." He looked over at John and smiled. "Things should get back to normal soon," he said as he felt greatly relieved. "When will my vault be fixed?"

"The team is making its rounds. It'll be within the next few months."

"Cool," Grant smiled. He felt happy, truly happy. He felt he had closure and answers to all the lingering questions. "I have other things to consider," he said as he thought of years and years of married life.

John laughed with his longtime friend as he clapped him on the back. "Cool, dude, very cool!"

* * * * * * *

Charlotte and Becker were passing by the room when they overheard the conversation. They had just come up from the basement where they had moved the clocks housing the royals. They looked at each other in concern. Both of them had sensed the powerful presences continuing to build. They were uneasy and helpless to know what to do next.

They were going to talk to Grant until they heard his comment to John about things returning to normal. The same thought passed between them, the wraith and the human that both cared deeply for this Keeper. *We can wait. Let him enjoy things for a time. Nothing can be done right now, anyway. When the time comes, we'll let him know our concerns.*